From The World of Strangers and Pilgrims

Book Two:

INTO SHADOW'S FIRE

SECOND EDITION

BY:
MARK CASTLEBERRY

SECOND EDITION

ISBN: 979-8-9853947-5-7 (Paperback)
ISBN :978-1-0881-5641-4 (E-Book)

Library of Congress Control Number: 2023910733

Any references to historical events, real people, or real places are used fictitiously. Names, characters, and places are products of the author's imagination.

Front cover image by Wonder.
Book design by Mark Castleberry.

Printed in the United States of America.

First printing edition 2022.

Strangers and Pilgrims Publishing
www.strangerspilgrims.com

TABLE OF CONTENTS

For my wife,
and my family and friends

There was a certain rich man, which was clothed in purple and fine linen, and fared sumptuously every day: And there was a certain beggar named Lazarus, which was laid at his gate, full of sores, And desiring to be fed with the crumbs which fell from the rich man's table: moreover the dogs came and licked his sores. And it came to pass, that the beggar died, and was carried by the angels into Abraham's bosom: the rich man also died, and was buried: And in hell he lift up his eyes, being in torments, and seeth Abraham afar off, and Lazarus in his bosom. And he cried and said, Father Abraham, have mercy on me, and send Lazarus, that he may dip the tip of his finger in water, and cool my tongue; for I am tormented in this flame.

    - Luke 16:10-24 KJV

CHAPTER ONE

Synoa

Six months after the battle over Bel Terra, the freighter Bird of Prey was coming closer to Synoa Station. The Republic and the Federation battleships had all disappeared. Other battleships were already being constructed at the Ikon shipyards to take their place. Soon, the Republic and the Federation would also be replaced. It had already started. What was needed now were the fuel rods to operate these new ships.

Bjorn Chelli's freighter pulled closer, throwing its search lights on top of the station. "Jenson," Bjorn began, "you and Phoss get some suits and helmets on and get ready to go over once when we find an airlock. We need to get this station working."

"Found it!" shouted Wade, the ship's pilot.

The ship slowed, and the lights lit up the airlock

leading into the station. A moment later, Jenson and Phoss climbed out of the lower airlock from the Bird of Prey and jumped down onto the space station itself. After they activated their magnetic boots Jenson pulled out a small box, connecting it to the coded airlock. He turned on the box, and it began finding the code to the entrance.

Several minutes passed before the outer airlock door unlocked and it could be opened. Once inside the station, both men had to turn on the lights on their helmets. "Okay, we're in," Jenson said into the open comms to the freighter.

"Alright, good, now go to the control room and get this station operating," Bjorn told them. "We got Shin here ready to hack into the system and get the tunnel to the lithium mines operating."

"Will do, boss," Jenson replied. Then he led the way toward the control room.

As they came close, he motioned for Phoss to head to the corridor leading to the upper level bridge control to connect the splicing chip for Shin. He continued straight and was soon inside the control room searching for the power panel. Soon he found the panel and followed the startup procedure. Lights began to flicker on and the computers slowly began to compute.

Above him on the bridge, Phoss began seeing the lights come on, and he immediately began looking for atmosphere controls. He found them and switched them on. The air recycling system clicked on, and within a few minutes he was able to remove his helmet. On his headset, he heard Jenson's voice telling him to find the splicing chip connection. The computer had many firewalls and passwords protecting it from anyone completely starting up the station without the proper codes.

Phoss pulled out the chip and plugged it into the computer system. "Okay," he announced over his comms, "Shin, do your stuff."

Jenson walked onto the bridge then, and as Shin hacked his way into the station's systems, he and Phoss decided to check out the rest of the station.

Back on board the Bird of Prey, Bjorn stood behind Shin watching him do his thing. "System is still booting itself up, so it might be a while before I can get started proper, sir."

"Don't rush it," Bjorn told him. "Better to get it done right."

Shin kept typing and he was slowly making progress.

Back on the station Jenson and Phoss continued to explore. They found the medical bay, with all the equipment missing. They knew someone had been hurt, and they had needed to be moved out. Phoss even found dried blood on the floor. Jenson reached the canteen and found dried food packets that had fallen on the floor when the gravity had been turned back on. It all needed a good cleaning before getting it back into proper use.

Back on board the freighter, the other members of the team, Kariss and Wade, were getting ready to check out the mining facility once the tunnel had been opened. After about an hour, a green beam shot out from the mining facility to the edge of the asteroid field behind the station. The beam then opened up into a ring that moved the surrounding asteroids slowly out from the space, creating a tunnel leading directly to the mining facility.

Bjorn contacted Jenson on the station. "We're heading to the facility. Stay on the station's bridge until we return. Shin says he has connected the tunnel controls back to the station. It should work now." Both Jenson and Phoss made their way slowly back to the bridge.

The mining facility was located on one of the largest asteroids in the field. It was actually where the lithium was first found, and was the first asteroid to be mined. As they were mining it, they began establishing the base there by carving out the loading bay and the smaller docking bays above.

Within many of the craters of the giant rock they had constructed large office complexes. Deep within the asteroid was Synoa City, a place where the workers and their families could live and enjoy life's pleasures. This way they would not have to leave their families behind on some world far away. After about a hundred years, Synoa Mining Facility had become a self-sufficient world of a sort. The field of the asteroids that surrounded the facility took up nearly half the system in a full dense globe, orbiting a gaseous planet that kept the field stable and together.

The mining facility had become the main source of lithium in the entire galaxy. It had also become the processing plant creating the fuel rods needed to fuel starships.

The freighter began moving slowly into the tunnel. The view from the inside of the tunnel was a glowing green, and the slow trip to the facility took nearly 20 minutes.

Once the Bird of Prey had left the field, the green tunnel subsided, giving the ship room to maneuver toward the facility. Automatic deflectors from the facility ran on the remaining power within, keeping the other rocks from crashing down on it.

Bjorn activated the comm. "Jenson, do you have control of the mining facility's docking bays?"

"Checking."

The docking bays' doors were located within several craters of the giant rock. The freighter came in close to one of the doors and waited. Located on a cliff-like area overlooking the bay doors were several black protrusions, which were a part of the facility itself.

Suddenly, outside lights came on around the mining facility, lighting up the rock, and Jenson's voice came back through the speakers. "Bay door one, now opening. It's all we got control of, sir. The rest is up to you."

Bjorn smiled. He could always count on Jenson. "Good job. Contact home base and tell Keiper to get his people out here and let's get this place up and running. We're going to need this lithium."

After the bay doors opened, the Bird of Prey landed

softly in the bay itself. The first order of business was restarting the gravity drive.

In addition to creating sufficient gravity, the gravity drive would also supply the basic electrical system. Once the giant batteries had been charged to full capacity, other systems could be manually turned on, like the oxygen generators. Under normal circumstances, oxygen was provided by several large gardens grown inside the rock. The garden was now dead, but the oxygen generators were there as a backup system for emergencies like this.

The facility had probably been abandoned soon after the battle over Bel Terra. Shutting down the mining facility had been done purposely. Someone seemed to know what was coming. Bjorn was glad they had gotten here before the residual power for the deflectors and start-up system had been completely depleted. Synoa was a major step in getting things going.

Bjorn looked over at Shin. "Are you able to hack your way in from here, or do we have to go in?"

"I can do it here, but it will take time," replied Shin. "Not all the systems are on, so I have to transfer power from one place to another, starting with the docks here, and keep moving inward. So the power here will get low."

"You can use ship's power if you need it," Bjorn told him.

Kariss walked in. "I want to go exploring," she said.

"Later," her boss answered. "We have plenty of time."

Twelve days later, the mining facility's power had been restored as fully as possible with the resources they had available. They contacted the station to inform them about the power, and Jenson responded by telling them that Keiper and his men had just arrived in their long-range transports. A few moments later, the green tunnel appeared. The three transport ships with the new facility crew emerged a short time later.

Bjorn met Keiper as he stepped off the transport. "This is a nice facility," Keiper said as they shook hands. They had originally met on Khair Din. He had also been brought there with the help of Mister Electrik.

"So how long do you think until you can get this place up and running steadily?" Bjorn asked him, and they both walked toward the internal living within the rock.

"We're going to have to check it out, see if things are

missing, check the supplies, things like that," Keiper replied. "Give me a couple of months, give or take several days."

Others poured from the three transports and headed straight into the bay, lining up as if they were in the military themselves. There, they received orders on where they were to work, based upon their personal traits and talents. A half an hour later, the place was buzzing again, and the mining facility would soon be up and running and more alive than ever.

Bjorn was contacted by Jenson several hours later. "Boss, station people are here. Phoss and I are ready to be picked up. I think we're more or less in the way now."

"Alright," Bjorn said. He knew things here were proceeding well. "I'll gather Wade and Kariss, and we'll head out soon. Good job out there."

"Thanks, boss," answered Jenson.

Bjorn found Keiper. "Keep me informed on the progress. We need this place up and running by the time our new battleships get off the assembly line."

"It will be ready," Keiper assured him.

CHAPTER TWO
Homeward Bound
Eleven and a half years later.

Nicolea Dan was awake. The FTL ship was heading back from Khair Din without the FTL drive. With the drive, it would have taken them two years to return, but it was going to take about a decade in lightspeed. Nicolea had spent most of the trip in his sleep pod. He had set it to wake him once a year, but Soshiana often woke him earlier.

Soshiana was monitoring the ship. The long journey was not as difficult for her, and as a bio-tek, the sleeping pods were unnecessary. She would wake Nicolea every few months and talk to him about her situation, and about her belief in and understanding of the Lord of Light. He would stay up for about a week talking with Soshiana, reading, and wandering the ship. He would even go down to the docking bay and explore the Chimera, the space yacht that the Godfather of the Galaxy, Thermonte Electrik, had built.

Now Nicolea was in his cabin alone with Lenok's satchel. Nicolea always spent some of his waking time looking over the things that the Prophet Warrior had left behind. Within the satchel he noticed that Lenok had carried multiple scrolls from his own life, as well as others which he had read and studied often. Soshiana, he knew, read some while he was sleeping. He sorted through them, and found one that seemed to come after the death of Kief Dan.

He opened the scroll the rest of the way and began to read.

And Lenok, son of Lesh, abode in New Galmesh for a time after the false religion of Dagon had crumbled and faded away from the city. The White Seraph appeared to him one evening as he meditated in his prayers.

"Lenok, son of Lesh, you have delivered this city from the shadow of Dagon quickly, and you will be rewarded with a moment of peace within yourself. You must stay in New Galmesh, and you are to walk to the main gates of the city every day of your peace, until you see three soldiers from the land of

Chalkydria, the dark land to the west. They will be looking specifically for you. You will go with them to Ashkeloth, to someone who will need your service, and who is under the protection of the Light."

And so, Lenok did as the White Seraph had told him, and kept his vigil every day for one year and three months.

Now in the city of Ashkeloth, there was a man named Gideon, who had a high position within the city hierarchy. The ruler of the land of Chalkydria was the Duke Sala Poden, who was an evil man that worshiped the idols of Pan. Duke Poden believed that he was a part of the royal family of Pan.

Gideon, as commander of the palace guards, was posted within the palace. However, when he was home, he was a believer and followed the ways of the Lord of Light. He held meetings in his home to teach the ways of the Lord of Light, but things were becoming difficult. Duke Poden had made a declaration that anyone caught worshiping the Lord of Light would be imprisoned, and perhaps even put to death.

Gideon continually prayed and sought direction from the Lord of Light, and one night as he slept the White Seraph appeared unto him. "Send three of your most trusted men to the city of New Galmesh in the land of Abelech," the White Seraph said. Standing near the gates will be a Prophet Warrior. His name will be Lenok, son of Lesh, and he will return to your home and help rid the kingdom of Ash from the rule of Pan. He will lead His people to their promised land."

So Gideon sent for three of his guards, also believers in the Lord of Light. He told them what the White Seraph had told him. Under the cover of night, the three guards set out toward New Galmesh to bring back the Prophet Warrior.

It was on the night of the second full moon in the month of Nonnen that Lenok, the Prophet Warrior, saw three men making their way toward the city of New Galmesh. He went out to meet with them.

They met outside the city gate, and camped just outside the wall, where several others lived in tents outside the city. The next morning, the three guards led Lenok toward the kingdom of Ash. The names of the guards were Stark, Manis, and Kanis.

Stark was the leader of these, and he spoke often to Lenok about the situation in Ash, and life in the city of Ashkeloth. Lenok learned that Duke Poden was ruling with an iron grip, and anyone that did not follow the worship of Pan was usually immediately killed and displayed in the center square. There were Children of the Light, Ghels, who were the chosen people of the Lord of Light, living in the kingdom of Ash, mostly as slave labor as they had been taken from the lower lands of Machonon. They were the ones being killed. Gideon and his three guards, according to Stark, had been converted by a Ghel and now worshiped the Lord of Light. The Ghel's name was Janik Kas. Janik Kas had been taken prisoner and tortured until he had converted the four men, who have since helped the Ghel people.

Within three days, they had reached the kingdom of Ash, and two days after that they had come upon the city of Ashkeloth. There Lenok was housed by a nearby family of the Ghel, and was asked to wait for Gideon to come to him. Lenok took the time to pray and worship the the Lord of Light with his fellow Ghel kin. For Lenok, son of Lesh, was of the Ghel people.

Three more days passed, before the man Gideon came to see Lenok. "What is your worry?" he asked Gideon as they sat and ate bread one evening.

"Duke Poden intends to issue a new decree, that states all Ghel people must begin to attend the worshiping of Pan before the next new moon, or they will be rounded up and set up in a public execution," Gideon told him. "I want to, so much, kill the duke with my bare hands."

"I will visit with this duke tomorrow and speak with him myself, to see if I can ascertain what his motives are."

"If you tell me the exact time, I shall announce you and help you deal with him," the captain of the guard said.

Lenok smiled. "You are a brave and loyal soul to the Ghel, but you must not let him know of your allegiance, not just yet. The Lord of Light has a plan and will deal with him *accordingly."*

Then, almost as an after thought, he said, "Perhaps he will use you as his servant for the dealing, my friend."

Then soon it was the time at which Lenok was to meet with Duke Poden. The duke was sitting on his throne dealing with his priests of Pan, when in came Lenok, son of Lesh, through the large wooden doors of the throne room. Standing next to the duke was Gideon at his usual spot. Several of the other guards, who did not know of the allegiance of Gideon, moved to remove Lenok from the room.

"Touch me not!" shouted Lenok as he burst into the room, holding up his staff and arms. The guards stopped. "Not until I have spoken the words I have been sent to speak," he continued.

Duke Sala Poden motioned for his priests to step on either side of the stranger, as he curiously watched the man walking in. "And what words does one use to a ruler of a country, after presenting himself so callously?"

"I bring a warning, that if you do not release the Ghel people from their servitude, this city of Ash will be smitten with fire, and all that remain within it."

Poden laughed. "A warning? A warning from who? And just who are you, audacious sir?"

"I am Lenok, Prophet Warrior of the Ghel people. The warning is from the one true God, the God of Light, not of

shadow and death as you tend to worship." Lenok was sure of his words, though they sounded prideful. It was not pride, but strength. "With the Lord of Light's help and power, I have taken the worship of Dagon away from New Galmesh just as the worship of Pan will be taken from Ashkeloth."

Duke Poden lingered in his thoughts for a moment. "So you are the one that restored the heresy of Light back to the capital city of Connacht."

"The Lord of Light has done that," replied Lenok, "I was but His servant." He glanced up at Gideon just standing there not moving.

An ease came across Gideon then, and he let things play out. He would trust the Lord of Light, and he would trust in Lenok.

Duke Poden just stared harshly at the Prophet Warrior. Then he shouted his orders to his guards, "Take a hold of that witch and bring me his staff, for if he is a true Prophet Warrior, that is where he holds his power!"

Two guards restrained Lenok, as another held a drawn sword at his throat. A fourth guard took Lenok's staff and brought it to his duke. Duke Poden broke the staff upon his own knee and handed it back to the guard.

Then he turned and spoke directly to Gideon. "Take this heretic and throw him into the lowest prison cell and chain him to the wall. At the rise of the next new moon when the Ghel begin to *worship me, I will execute their hope before their eyes."*

Gideon led the way and they took Lenok below, to the lowest part of the palace, to the dungeon there, and chained him. Lenok just smiled and said to him, "Just pray for me and for guidance. All will come to pass as it should for His glory."

Gideon just nodded and said, "I will return every day until all is revealed."

Lenok just smiled and agreed.

Many times Jon had also woken up from the sleep pods and had found Nicolea and Soshiana in the kitchen of the FTL talking. Soshiana seemed to mostly be asking questions, and Nicolea was answering them. He would come in and get himself something to eat and sit with them, not saying a word. He would just listen, taking in what they both had to say.

He would speak every now and again in greeting and other such trivial words, but not about the Light, as he knew it. He had seen things in his travels with Nicolea that put his thinking process to the test. Yes, he believed there was a God, the Lord of Light, and His son Iosa, but he never got much into religion like other friends he once knew. Many of his old friends had stayed behind on his home world and had lived a normal life, which included worshiping the Lord of Light at the local church. But Jon had been different.

He wanted a more exciting, thrilling life. He joined the local military and then the special services, where he became a planetary Agent of the Republic. Then, with several years of service under his belt, he became one of the galactic Agents of the Republic, which gave him jurisdiction over all Republic worlds. He would often wonder, now, just what shape the Republic was in. Would it be the same? Would it be a different way of life? He wished he had gotten in touch with the president before they had left.

All he had now, while he was awake, was to listen to Nicolea preach, or teach as he had put it, to Soshiana, a bio-tek. Mister Electrik's bio-tek of all things. Could the bio-tek comprehend what was being said to her? After waking up so many times and listening to the question and answer session between them, be began to wonder if she really could comprehend what believing in the Lord of Light meant. In fact, he was beginning to understand it more himself just by listening. After all the things he had done in the past, could he become a Child of the Light and have a place in the Great Paradise that waited in the end?

As always, after getting himself something to eat, and telling the others he was heading back into the pod for a while, he would go back to sleep and wake up again to basically do the same thing. But he noticed that after a while he started to remember dreams that he had while sleeping in the pods. He also realized that he had started becoming more tolerant to Soshiana's questions and Nicolea's answers. He was also starting to look forward to listening to them talk. So much so, that he began staying up longer and interacting with them more.

This continued, until Nicolea suddenly woke him up from the pod without an explanation. "Time to leave the FTL."

Still a bit unsure of himself, he said, "What is it?"

"We made it back into known space," Nicolea said, and Jon noticed his beard for the first time. "It sent out a distress signal automatically, and we don't want to be found unless we know who has found us."

"Gotcha," Jon replied. Then he said, "You grew a beard. How long you been awake?"

"Last two years," Nicolea replied. He stroked the fur on his face. "You like it?"

"Somehow it fits ya."

They made their way quickly to the docking bay,

where Soshiana was waiting by the Chimera. "Hurry," she said. "I know for a fact that Mister Electrik had this ship built so it could not be tracked, so they will not find us once we leave." The two men looked at her strangely. "You know, criminal activities and all."

"Well, that's one thing good he did for us," Jon said, as he climbed aboard.

Within minutes, the Chimera lifted out of the docking bay of the FTL, and flew away from it just as fast as it could. Soshiana had timed the FTL's computer to shut itself off, and soon it became cold and began to just drift. The only thing it had working was the distress call.

CHAPTER THREE
Dust Expanded

The winds stirred the earth as they blew. Walking through the desert, the unknown man headed toward the town of Dust, which was named after the colony world of Dust. The town of Dust had been in existence for nearly thirty years and was a booming town. It was also a rough town, and men openly carried hand held weapons on their person. Life was tough there. There was mining in the Sharai Mountains, into which Dust was nestled on three sides. Panning for gold in the river was popular with newcomers to the town. Much of the gold was spent in the local saloons and brothels.

As the unknown man made his way into the town, with the wind still stirring up the dirt around him, he was greeted by many drunken women trying to sell him their services. He looked around and watched the inhabitants of the town, who all seemed drunk.

It was morning, and the sun had been up for several hours now. The local law was a sheriff named Bolen. He saw the stranger, whose face was covered with a dirty brown handkerchief. In fact, everything he was wearing was a murky brown, except for his black boots and a loose-fitting shirt. The vest he wore was that dirty brown, as was the worn, wide-brimmed hat on his head.

Sheriff Bolen walked out into the middle of the dirty street and walked toward the new man. "Can I help you?" On his hip was an old blaster pistol he had gotten many years ago.

The unknown man carried no known weapons. None that Bolen could see, anyway. "Mister, I asked you a question."

"I heard you," the man replied. "Do you approve of the evil going on in this town?"

The sheriff chuckled. "This is just life here," he said. "We're a colony, and we make our own laws. The rest of the galaxy has no jurisdiction here."

The unknown man looked around. "I'm looking for a righteous man."

"You're in the wrong town, Mister," the sheriff chuckled. Looking around, the sheriff noticed others watching his transaction with this man. The unknown man had also noticed. The sheriff said, "Listen, partner, where is your ship? Nothing has landed at the spaceport in several days."

The unknown man just looked at him. There was something about the stranger's eyes; it was the way he looked at him. The sheriff began to get nervous. This man didn't seem right. He never answered him, but just stood there looking at Sheriff Bolen.

"I don't know any righteous man," he finally said to the man. "Do you know for sure he is here?"

The man looked up over the sheriff's head, looking around the town. "He is here." Then a moment of strange silence, before he spoke again. "This town contains so much evil. You need to deal with it, Sheriff."

Bolen breathed in. "I didn't catch your name."

Nothing.

Bolen spoke again. "You can check the registry at the spaceport for your righteous man. Then you need to get out. We don't want your kind here. You understand, Mister?"

Just then, a drunken woman strolled out of the saloon and saw the sheriff. "Hey Sheriff!" she called out. "Those guys are at it again!"

"I'll be right there, Marta," he called back. Then, to

the man, he said, "I hope you're planning to follow our laws. Don't do anything that will cause me to hunt you down. Me and my deputies will be keeping our eyes on you, and you won't know who they are."

Then after another look into those strange, old eyes, Sheriff Bolen turned and followed the woman as she went back into the saloon.

Toward the base of the mountains there sat several houses. They had been there for years, worn and in different stages of decay. However, there was one of the houses further back that looked much newer. Jesse Boone lived there with his wife, Abagael, and his daughter Maggie. Maggie was twelve years old, but they had all lived there for just four years. Jesse worked as a miner up in the hills near the river valley. He wasn't well-liked in the town, for he didn't live like the rest of the township.

This was the house the unknown man began walking to. The man knew there were eyes upon him, and that there would be much grief for his choice of destination. There was, in fact, one man, one of the drunkards, that slowly stood up. He watched the unknown man move toward Jesse Boone's house. He, himself, moved as quick as he could, and made his way across the street and into the saloon. Inside, one man was dead on the floor, and one close to death was slumped in a chair. Sheriff Bolen stood at the bar with a drink in his hand.

The drunkard's name was Hossa. He made his way near the sheriff. Bolen took a drink and turned around. "That stranger made his way straight to Jesse Boone's house, Sheriff."

Bolen remembered who the man was looking for: a righteous man. "What's that got to do with me, Hossa?"

"Maybe this stranger is the law, I mean, maybe the real law."

The sheriff looked at him sternly and considered backhanding him for a moment. Hossa continued. "I don't mean to say you ain't the law, sheriff, I'm just saying … you know, the galaxy law."

Sheriff Bolen knew what the drunken man was talking about. The stranger hadn't answered his questions, or even given him his name. He finished off his drink and turned around. He saw several men who worked for him among the other customers in the saloon. "Okay, boys," he shouted across the room. "Gather the others, we gonna find out what this stranger is up to. Maybe we can turn him over to the Empire for some cash."

Meanwhile, the unknown man had knocked on the Boone door. Jesse opened the door. The man spoke quickly and first. "Are you Jesse Boone?"

Jesse nodded that he was. "Yes."

The man stepped through the door and closed it behind him, moving Jesse back a bit. His wife came from around the corner to see who their visitor was. "I am Gideon. You are to leave this town and head north to where an oasis of green waits for you."

Jesse had never seen this man before, but he instantly knew that he was to be obeyed. Jesse and his family were followers of the Lord of Light. Their belief gave them peace, but it also made them criminals according to the Empire's laws. Dust was not a friendly town, it was a place people of criminal tendencies went to hide. That meant it was also a good place for Jesse and his family to hide.

After hearing the man's words, Jesse and his family began to quickly gather the essentials in bags. "Are you coming with us?" he asked the man.

"I will make sure that you safely depart," said Gideon, "but I have work here in Dust."

Jesse looked into the man's eyes. They were old, ancient, and Jesse knew those eyes had seen much. He would never know just how much Gideon had seen.

Soon there was a knock on the door. It was the sheriff. "Jesse Boone, this is Sheriff Bolen. Send us the stranger, or you will face the mob."

Jesse took a glance out the window. Not only was it the sheriff, but it looked as if every disreputable member of society was there as well. In Dust that was quite a large number. His wife and daughter came back into the room after getting everything together they would need for the journey north.

Then Gideon said to them, "Regardless of what you hear or see after you leave, do not feel grief. This town is evil, and this town must be dealt with. Trust the Light of the Lord to guide you."

The knock on the door had gotten stronger and louder. Jesse took his family and headed out the back door. The man reached out and opened the front door after he was sure the family had gotten out safely. He looked up and around above the townsfolk's heads as if breathing in the air around them. He knew, then, that the Boone family had not been followed.

Put out, the sheriff grabbed the man by his vest and flung him to the ground. He then kicked him several times until Gideon was lying in the dusty street. Finally,

Sheriff Bolen asked, "Who are you, mister? You tell us now. Are you with the Empire?"

The man wiped the blood from a small cut on his face. "Your Empire means nothing," was his only answer. Slowly, he began to stand up. "There is evil in this town of Dust, and to dust, this town will return."

Everyone laughed, even the sheriff. He pulled his blaster pistol from the holster hanging at his side. "And what does that mean, mister? I tell you what it means. It means you got no idea who you're dealing with. We could just kill you, or maybe we should just hand you over to the Empire. Is there a reward?"

The man reached up inside his left sleeve and pulled out a silver rod with his right hand. He shook his right hand, and the rod grew into a silver staff. The crowd of townsfolk were somewhat taken aback, but the sheriff extended his gun outward, pointing it at the man's chest. "What are you doing?" Bolen demanded to know.

"This is the staff of the Lord of Light given to me to destroy this town of sin and evil. Darkness reigns here, and it will end. I am Gideon, the destroyer of evil, sent by the one true God, the Lord of Light, to turn this town back to dust."

Sheriff Bolen fired his weapon at the man.

Somehow, he missed. Gideon raised the staff up high, then brought it down, straight and hard, to the ground.

Jesse and his family had reached the second tier of the mountain. A path there led deeper into the mountain valley behind. Just as his wife and daughter had stepped over onto the trail, they heard a loud, deafening boom. Abagael grabbed Maggie and fell forward onto the path, thinking it would protect her. Jesse jumped onto the path and turned around, waiting for a fight. He thought maybe someone had followed them. Instead, he saw a rising cloud of dust.

A moment later dust and wind rushed by him, settling farther along the path. Some of it settled on his wife as she lay on the path holding Maggie. Jesse couldn't see what had actually happened to Dust, and he never went back to find out.

From the cloud of lingering dust surrounding the town, a single man walked out into the desert lands. He was once again an unknown man, a man no one knew.

It was a screeching sound that woke Jesse up a few mornings later. He opened his eyes and saw a krakadon standing there looking back. The scale-covered creature stared at him with black eyes and let out another screeching sound, almost like it was trying to communicate.

Jessie sat up. His wife and daughter were still sleeping in the tent behind him, but he had slept outside, for the tent was too small for all of them to use. The krakadon stood about eight feet high. He knew about these creatures, and knew they had a palatable flavor. He had never eaten krakadon before, but when you are hungry, everything tastes good. This type of krakadon was a sand krakadon. Sand krakadons could not fly, like their larger kin. Instead, they used their strong legs to run fast.

He reached down to his hip, and pulled out his small sidearm. The krakadon spread its wings and moved back a bit. Before the creature could run off, Jesse shot the creature in the head, and it fell dead.

The sound of the shot woke his wife, and she came out from the tent. "What is going on?" she asked, not knowing what to expect.

Jesse turned back and smiled. "Don't worry about it," he told her. "I just got us some breakfast. It will be ready in a couple of hours."

"How much farther do we have to go?"

"There is a fertile canyon north of here. We'll find

more food there I hope."

"Will we be able to get off this world?"

He shrugged. "I don't know if there is another town anywhere. We can only hope there are others here."

After breakfast, they traveled north for several more days, eating what they had brought with them, and killing other small desert animals along the way. One day as they were walking along just hours before the sun was to go down, they heard a loud call coming from the sky. It was so loud, it frightened Maggie.

Jesse looked up and saw the large krakadon flying overhead. This was a mire krakadon. These creatures were not covered in scales like their smaller cousins. The larger ones were mostly covered in black or brown feathers, with multicolored smaller feathers covering the belly. As Jesse squinted his eyes, narrowing his view, he saw that this beast was saddled, with a rider on it.

The beast circled several times, then flew further north. Jesse pulled out a pair of field glasses and tried to see the rider closer, but it was too far. He did however see a hint of mountains and trees ahead. Was this why he was told to head north?

"I think we are almost there," he announced to his family.

"Where is there?" his wife asked.

"We're going to find out," Jesse replied.

They continued moving north toward the oasis of green mountains ahead. Slowly they encountered a few weeds, then thicker bushes of greenery, some with flowers. Then the trees, smaller ones at first, then the thick trunks appeared. Then Jesse and his family stopped, standing in front of a giant boulder, and on that boulder was a man. The man was wearing a dark-colored uniform of some kind, and his nose and mouth were covered with a scarf.

"So, what is your story and who are you?" the man asked.

"My family and I have come from the town of Dust, which I believe has been totally destroyed." Jesse told the man.

"We know," answered the man. "What we don't know is what happened. Can you tell us that?"

"A man came to us, his name was Gideon, and it was him who has destroyed the town," Jesse answered. "He saved our lives and sent us up this way, heading north to this oasis on the desert planet."

For a moment there was silence. Then the man asked

again, "Who are you?"

"My name is Jesse Boone. This is my wife and daughter. We are just simple colonists."

Another silent moment. Jesse's wife leaned in whispering in his ear, but before he could answer her question, the man spoke to them again. "Are you kin to Grand Admiral Solomon Boone?"

Jesse was taken aback. "My brother's name is Solomon, and last I heard he was an admiral in the Republic Navy. I have not heard from him for over twelve years. We thought he died in the battle over Bel Terra."

"Follow me," the man said, and he jumped down from the back of the boulder and walked around the giant rock to where Jesse and his family were standing. He motioned for them to follow and then stepped onto a nearby trail that was hidden by the brush. Jesse and his family followed the man. They went deeper into the jungle-like forest and finally into a small cave. There they realized the man had revealed that this was an entrance to something bigger. A doorway slid open showing the corridors inside.

Standing there waiting for them was Jesse's brother, Solomon Boone, now the grand admiral of this, whatever it was. Solomon's words explained it. "Welcome to the Union, little brother. I am very glad you and your family are with us and safe."

"We thought you were dead?" Jesse said, and hugged him as a brother.

"Just in hiding for the moment. At the battle of Bel Terra, Grand Admiral Shepherd knew what was coming. He had this set up long before the battle. He sent us here to grow secretly," Solomon explained as they moved inside the corridor.

"That was twelve years ago, Sol," Jesse said.

Solomon smiled. "And we have grown. And your big brother is the new grand admiral. All we need now is a fleet to use against the Empire."

As they walked through the base, they continued to talk. Jesse asked, "Don't you have any ships?"

"We have a few, here and there, but not nearly enough to fight back. It is harder to accumulate those things. But we believe that the Lord of Light will see us through." Solomon welcomed his brother and his family into the fold.

CHAPTER FOUR

Rise Of Sorrow

Thermonte Electrik sat nearly alone in the giant hall within the palace on the world of Bel Terra. Only one other man was with him, and that was Andrelus Pan. He was standing some distance from Thermonte, reading a report he had given him.

"How do you enjoy being the emperor of the galaxy?" Andrelus mocked him. Thermonte didn't catch the meaning.

"Not what I thought it would be like," admitted the ex-criminal, now serving as the galactic emperor of the Pagonic Imperium. It was like any other empire, but it was also something else, and Thermonte knew this.

The report Andrelus was reading told him of the border search for an incoming ship, which was to return soon. The Empire had been established several years ago, and it had been longer than that since the ship had gone out beyond known space.

"I understand you are building yourself a throne for the inner courtyard," he said to Thermonte.

"It's for the Imperial Tribute coming up this next year. I think it would be nice for the people to actually see their emperor, not just to see him on a giant screen somewhere."

Andrelus smiled. "I am all for it, my emperor, all for it."

Thermonte liked it when someone referred to him as emperor, even if it was Andrelus. Promises had been made in the past, and it all had paid off. It made him think of the old days, and all that it took to get here.

"I'm heading out," Andrelus told him, handing him the report. "Still trying to find a way to bring Phaleg here. I'll keep in touch. You can use Chelli if you need anything." Then he left, leaving Thermonte alone.

Thermonte didn't even look at the report. Instead, he just thought back to his past. He was proud of his climb to the top, though he still had some disappointments. But even so, it was a well-thought-out plan. After a moment, he stood up and walked back into his personal chambers.

After restarting the lithium mines at Synoa, and

getting the processing plant working again, Bjorn Chelli and his crew had found themselves back on Bel Terra in the capital city of New Galmesh. Already their plan had been put into motion. With the chaos of the missing leaders of both the Republic and the Federation, immediate elections had to be held to gain new leadership to help rebuild their societies from the wreckage caused by the Bathshe War.

Several years before the Bathshe War, a new political party, the Pagonic Party, had risen up within the Republic. They slowly rose in popularity, offering equality for all citizens and unity with the Federation. Bjorn Chelli and his men were active participants in this party, working behind the scenes. The Pagonic Party was now on the ballot for the emergency election.

The election took place almost eight months after the battle over Bel Terra, but while the election was going on, it seemed that the Bathshe had returned and started another war. With the Pagonic Party in control of Synoa Mining Facility and the Ikon Shipyards, they were ready to defend the civilized galaxy. For the next year and a half, the Second Bathshe War raged on.

Then something happened that changed the war. One man came forward and took control of the Pagonic military might, and fought back the Bathshe. This man's name was Thermonte Electrik. The battles he won and the way he conducted himself began to erase people's image of him as a gangster. After fighting long, hard battles against the Bathshe for four months, Thermonte Electrik brokered a peaceful solution with them. Soon, the Bathshe had left both territories, and Thermonte was hailed as a hero. When the next Republic election took place, he was the Pagonic Party's candidate for Republic president.

Thermonte was also a hero with the Federation. Soon after being elected, Thermonte brought peace between the two factions. In fact, it was only about a year later that the Federation joined the Republic, and through political talks and meetings, and rewriting the constitutions of the two territories, it was decided to combine the two into one. After a few more attacks from rogue Bathshe, and a political rebellion of little consequence, the Empire was formed. Later, it would be officially called the Pagonic Imperium and the hero of the war was none other than Thermonte Electrik, and he became the empire's first ruler.

A ministry council was formed just beneath the ruling power to help govern the empire. It was under this ministry that certain programs and laws were formed to tighten the grip on the people. Minor rebellions rose up and were put to rest by the new Pagonic military and Local forces.

Under the guise of protecting the rights of certain groups of people, the council created the Molokan Way, a way to destroy a birth before the birth took place. Their thinking was that if they did not have to see an actual child, and if the child was not actually born yet, then the child was not actually alive. Another new order, a religious compliance act, stated that all Churches of Light and other such organizations must comply with the Imperium. No one was to worship, unless they worshiped the Imperium emperor, Thermonte Electrick. The religion was being adapted, with Thermonte in place as god.

This led to underground churches being formed, even as the prior temples and churches of Light were systematically being destroyed from both within and without. True believers met in each other's homes in small groups at different hours to avoid being caught.

Within two years, the Pagonic Imperium was ruling the empire with fear. They had created a new galactic way of life, a "New Society," with the Imperium as the sole source of authority. Many people just accepted this new way of life, but there were others who refused.

The Imperial palace was the center of the giant capital city of Bel Terra. This is where Thermonte Electrik both lived and worked, conducting all of his activities hidden away from the rest of the galaxy. Many hated him now, displeased with the way the Empire had turned out. Many wondered if he was really in charge, or if it was the ministry council that actually ruled.

Thermonte Electrik finished off his glass of whiskey, straight from his home world of Chotis. If his whiskey wasn't from Chotis, then it wasn't good whiskey. He wouldn't mind going back there at some point. In front of him was a giant tray of food, and around his waist, the years of being an emperor were accumulating.

"You've gotten way too fat." It was Bjorn Chelli; he had just come back from a mission.

"I've been getting fat long before I knew any of you," the former crime lord replied. Now, he was the face of the Pagonic Imperium. "I once knew someone else who would have said something similar to me." His mind shifted for a brief moment to Soshiana.

"Anyway," Bjorn said, "I just came to tell you that we found the FTL ship. It finally made it back to sensor range."

This news seemed to perk up Thermonte. He might get a chance to see Soshiana again. She had been the most loyal person he had ever known. She was loyal to a T. "Are you tracking it?"

"Yea, we're about to head out and retrieve it."

"Bring back anyone alive to me."

Bjorn nodded. "Of course." He turned and walked out. He hated having to answer to this fat man.

Thermonte leaned back in his chair. He would finally be able to see his good friend, his good and most trusted friend, Soshiana.

Bjorn Chelli was in command of a large cargo ship called the Padinger. In one of the holds of the ship sat his personal freighter. Along with his personal crew, others had been added on board the Padinger for the sole purpose of finding the FTL ship, which had just re-entered known space. Now looking out of the bridge viewport, Bjorn watched as the FTL ship floated helplessly ahead of them.

Only his personal crew would be going into the derelict ship, looking around and trying to activate it. The other members of his team would be ready to help bring the FTL into the other empty hold.

Phoss and Kariss entered the FTL after they had come in close enough. They had jumped down onto its outer hull-, and then opened it up like a can of meat. After they entered the ship, Kariss turned and placed a static cover over the newly formed hole to make an airtight seal. The green glow and even hum indicated the connection was secure.

With weapons drawn, they both made their way slowly throughout the ship. They found the gathering place, where Nicolea and Soshiana used to talk about the Lord of Light. They never knew that, for the area was empty, barren, and cold. They moved further back and found the large, empty docking bay. They did find evidence that another ship had been there, but they had all known that in advance.

They had moved back into the living quarters of the ship, and found where Nicolea had his own personal room, while he was awake and reading the scrolls. Next to that room, they found the room where sleeping pods lay empty; their lids were still opened. In here, they moved slowly like they had done in the docking bay, but they found nothing. Different loose objects had been floating around, because the gravity had not yet been re-established, but that was to be expected.

After exploring the other rooms in the living area, including the dining hall and the galley, they made their way to the engine room in hopes of getting the power back on. Everything seemed normal.

"Everything looks good here," Kariss spoke. "Let's head up to the bridge and connect the splicing chip, and hand it over to Shin."

Phoss nodded his agreement. They moved on, moving slowly just in case someone was still hiding on board.

"How is it going over there?" they heard Bjorn's voice asking over their earpieces. "Find anything yet?"

"Everything seems to be intact and in working order," was Kariss' reply. "We're heading to the bridge to plug in."

"Check the fuel while you're at it. We may have to tow her in."

That is when Phoss chirped in. "I checked while we were in the back. There might be a little, but I don't think it will make it on its own."

"Alright," Bjorn answered. "I'll get the others here ready to tow her in on this end. Once you get the chip connected, get outside to start connecting the cables."

"Understood, sir," Phoss replied as he followed Kariss to the bridge.

On the bridge, nothing was found that particularly stuck out, and even connecting the splicing chip was easy. Kariss did find a notepad with the word "Alexeena" written on it, but she thought nothing of it and put it away in her suit pocket. She could always use a good notepad.

When the chip was placed and partial power had been turned on, the word was given. "We're heading on the outside," Kariss said to Bjorn. "Give us about fifteen minutes."

Phoss quickly checked the fuel. "I was right," he said. "Nearly out of fuel."

Before they had actually gotten outside, full power had been re-established. Kariss and Phoss could leave from one of the air-locks. As the ship was slowly being filled with oxygen, Phoss and Kariss were heading back outside in order to connect the tow cables being extended from the second cargo hold on the Padinger.

Moving slowly in space across the hull of the FTL, Phoss and Kariss finally made it to where they would connect the cables on the front of the ship. The derelict ship would not fit completely into the hull, so they would have to pull it in as close as possible, and leave the cargo doors open. That meant that the crew members working inside the cargo hold would also have to wear pressure suits.

As they waited for the cables to reach them, Shin began to search the ship's computer for information.

After about thirty minutes, he found what he was looking for. "So," he started to tell what he had found after Bjorn had come up behind him. "This ship's new FTL rocket engines are not actually on here. They were blown off, which accounts for this ship taking so long to return."

"What about the survivors?" Bjorn asked. "Thermonte made a point saying his bio-tek girl, Soshiana, would be here?"

"There was another, smaller ship on board."

"Yea, his majesty", he mocked, "said his private yacht would be in there as well."

Shin nodded. "With the fuel as low as it is, they more than likely left on that."

"Just download it all and we'll check it later," he told Shin.

The FTL ship had been successfully pulled into the second cargo hold, as much as was possible, and they headed away to the Imperial shipyards, formerly known as the Ikon shipyards.

"So what are you going to tell his majesty?" asked Kariss, once they had all sat down to eat their meal.

"You mean the fat man," Bjorn said, and grinned. "I will tell the fool the truth. His little girlfriend took off with his ship. Maybe she is not as loyal as he thinks she is."

They all chuckled. They knew Thermonte Electrik, emperor of the galaxy, was nothing but a fool. They all thought of him that way. They had to do what he told them, they knew, but they also knew the truth. They were like that with all leadership. The only leader they had any respect for and truly reported to was Andrelus Pan. The man behind the emperor. Andrelus was a true leader.

As the Padinger left from where they found the FTL, just seven hours away in the opposite direction, the Chimera headed slowly into the outer colony worlds, hoping to find some sort of civilization.

Thermonte was almost alone nearly every day. He had his memories of his rise to power. To him, it was a long and hard journey, and now he had finally reached it, and more. He could do anything now, and do it legally, without repercussion. His thoughts always seemed to travel back to his mother. He had loved her, and had always wanted to make her proud of him. She had achieved one thing she was proud of him for, before she had died.

She had gotten him married.

He had always wanted to bring his mother out of the poor district of Cinder, for he had always loved his mother. He had nothing but fond memories of her. He remembered purchasing land east of Necros. It was thickly wooded and was nestled within the misty mountains of Demorn, with a beautiful crystal lake at the base of the surrounding mountains. He was building a large home here, with his own personal docking bay within the mountain itself to host his yacht and several other smaller ships if needed.

He had brought her to that location on several occasions, and she was always smiling and was glad that her only son was doing well in life.

"You know, I told my friend Edith about you," she told him. "You know Edith, she goes to my church."

Thermonte had nodded. "I know her mom. You've introduced us several times." He was smiling. At first he thought she had a touch of dementia, but after a while, it was clear she was just happy to see him. He hadn't come around much.

"Anyway," she continued, "Edith has a niece who is staying with her named Anna, and she will be at church tomorrow and you will meet her at lunch."

"Mother, are you trying to set me up again?" he asked her. She had done it to him several times. She wanted him married and starting a family. She wanted grandchildren.

"You're building a home, Thermonte. A wife will give you stability," his mother said.

"Mother," he began.

She pointed her finger up at his face. "You will behave and be polite, won't you?" she asked. "She is a nice girl."

Thermonte was smiling. He knew his mother meant well; she was so old-fashioned. "I will behave, mother."

He had married that niece, who had been the only women he had ever loved. Oh, how he had loved Anna, and she had loved him back. After his mother's death, which hit him hard, Thermonte seemed to spend more time working and extending his syndicate throughout the Republic. Anna Electrik, along with her children, Thoran and Alexeena, disappeared. Thermonte had found a note telling him she had walked out on him and their marriage.

He sent one of his associates out to go find them, but he came up empty. It nearly broke him. It was at that point that Thermonte Electrik took up drinking heavily.

His son, Thoran, came back into the picture many years later and joined his father in the business, but he would never hear from his wife and daughter again.

Thermonte Electrik finished his latest glass of whiskey. Chotis always had the best whiskey. He just sat outside on one of the many balconies in the palace, and watched the comings and goings of the outside world. He hoped Soshiana would come back to him. He did miss her and wished she were here. She would fix everything for him.

CHAPTER FIVE
Reunion

The Chimera moved slowly among the stars of space. Soshiana was in the pilot's chair, and according to her, they were moving just within the edge of known galactic space. A blip appeared on the radar. She called her new friends up onto the small bridge. Nicolea and Jon both leaned down to look at the radar screen.

"You think they'll recognize this ship?" Nicolea asked Jon, knowing they were looking at an older Republic battleship. The readout had confirmed that much.

Jon smiled. "Probably, since this is a gangster's ship." They watched it for a little bit longer. "My question is, have they seen us?"

"Yes, they have," Soshiana piped in.

The radar pinged, and they watched as the battleship icon on the screen turned toward them. "What do you want to do?" Nicolea asked him.

"We'll see who they really are," Jon replied, standing back up, waiting.   He knew Republic standard procedure.

As the battleship closed in on them, and became visible out the viewport, the communications came to life. "Starship Chimera, this is the battleship Condor, please provide us with your destination and your reason for being in this sector."

To his shipmates, Jon said, "I don't remember that battleship name?"

"It's been twelve years since we left, remember," Nicolea reminded him.

Jon nodded. He sat down at the comms and spoke clearly into the mic. "We are looking for Republic space. Is this Republic space?"

There was a strange silence, and it took a few moments before the Condor replied. It wasn't what they had expected. "Chimera, your transponder code has not been seen or used in many years, so prepare to be boarded."

That was a new voice. Something about it. Jon seemed to know that voice. The woman's voice seemed to be in charge. But it was slightly different. *Could it be?*

Jon wondered.

"Should I run?" Soshiana asked, her hands on the thrust control.

Nicolea had never done his job as part of the Protectorate for the Federation in space, only on planets. He would travel from world to world to take care of government business, but never in space. They had other agencies for that. Now that he seemed to retire himself from his Protectorate duties, missing for twelve years, he had made himself a Prophet Warrior, taking the place of Lenok, who had died on the shadow world. He too was looking at Jon for an answer to this dilemma.

"No," assured Jon. "Let them board. I think I know that voice."

Soshiana removed her hand from the thrust control, and shut the engine down. They waited until the ship had been grappled, which meant they were being hauled into a separate docking bay. Jon knew it was specifically for troop boarding. There was no making a run for it now. Then all three of them moved to the yacht's main hatch to await the knock on the door.

It didn't take long for the knock to come.

Soshiana reached over and punched in the code to

the entrance and the door slid open. The face behind that voice was the first face Jon saw, and right away he knew who it was. Saffron Baye, his first love. Her long dark hair was pulled up in a military-style fashion with many streaks of grey weaving in and out of it. Her face didn't hold the youth he remembered, but was now a dozen years older than himself. He then suddenly realized just how long he had been gone.

"It's about time you got back, Jon Vega," she said quickly, grinning slightly.

He noticed her uniform. It looked a little like a Republic Navy admiral uniform, but the insignia was different. She noticed the look on his face and replied based on it. "The Republic no longer exists, Jon." She noticed Nicolea standing behind him and she also said, "Neither does the Federation."

"What?" That was Jon.

"Follow me, and we'll talk," she told them. They followed behind her closely, followed themselves by troops in similar uniforms.

She continued. "Do you remember the political party calling themselves the Pagonic Party, which never got much attention?"

"Yea sure, a little bit."

She stopped and turned around and looked at him. "They are now in control, and it's their empire we fight against. Apparently, Grand Admiral Shepherd knew this was coming, and sent instructions on what to do next."

Jon remembered back to the battle above Bel Terra. "Shepherd is dead. I watched his ship burn as it came down."

Saffron nodded. "I know. There is much more. You'll be told more, once you three get debriefed."

She continued walking, the others followed. Jon asked, "Who is in charge? Norris, Brande, who?"

They followed Saffron into a conference room, and she offered them chairs to sit around the table in the middle of the room. They took a seat, and she began to give answers. "Norris is no longer in charge, but he does help with the fight. General Brande was captured by the Pagonic Empire and is currently being held in the Black Star Prison, along with our spiritual leader, Bishop Cas Barnes. The one you will need to speak to back at base is Grand Admiral Solomon Boone."

Jon thought for a moment. "I have never heard of him."

"Shepherd appointed him in his instructions to follow in his stead," she replied. "We have done several attacks on the Pagonic Navy and on some of their military targets. But with limited ships and such, we haven't gotten very far."

She looked behind Jon, where Nicolea sat. He was now wearing the clothing of the Prophet Warrior. His bag and staff had been left behind on the Chimera. Nicolea was holding his hand in the air, waiting to be noticed. She noticed him and gave him her attention.

"What about Prime Minister Lamet?" he asked her. "Last I heard he was left in critical condition from the battle over Deveron."

"I remember," she answered. She did remember speaking to him back at the Synoan base. "And just to let you know, he is still with us."

A sigh of relief came from Nicolea. Lamet was someone Nicolea had looked up to. He was someone he would do almost anything for back in the day when he was a Protector.

"He is not in the best of health, so all he does is advise in different situations. He'll be happy to see you," she smiled. To the others, she said, "You guys will be told more once we reach the home base. We're heading there now."

"Where is home base?" Jon asked.

"The colony world of Dust."

Then she turned her attention to Soshiana. She remembered her from her and Jon's visit to Electrik's home on Chotis so long ago. "You worked for Thermonte Electrik, correct?"

Soshiana seemed to straighten up. "I did. He left me alone. I do not work with him any longer."

Saffron looked around at the others as they watched her. She said, "I thought Electrik went with you guys to this shadow world."

"He did."

With a look of confusion on her face, she asked, "Then how has he become the royal leader of the Pagonic Empire? He is the one that seems to be in charge."

Anger began to rise inside of Jon; everyone knew how he felt about him. Soshiana placed a hand on his arm, and they both looked into one another's eyes. They had both been through a lot, and had grown closer together as friends and closer to the Lord of Light, thanks to Nicolea.

As Jon stared into Soshiana's eyes, his feeling of hatred began to subside. He knew it was in the hands of God now. How it would be handled, he did not know, but he knew God had a plan.

"How long before we get there?" Nicolea asked.

"We're very close, actually," Saffron told him. "Couple of hours. I need you guys to stay in this room, if you don't mind. It's protocol," she explained. Then she smiled and said, "Welcome to the Union of Light."

Then she left, and they sat around the table. All felt the relief of being found and reaching civilization, but what kind of civilization, they had no idea. They talked about the possibilities for the duration of their trip to Dust.

Thermonte was getting ready for bed. Servants were around him helping him into his sleeping gown and getting his garments ready for the morning. The entire process took nearly half an hour, and when the servants left, Thermonte simply pulled back the covering of the bed and slowly climbed into it, pulling the covering back up around his chest. He left the light on as he just lay there thinking. His mind was on Soshiana, who was basically the only one he could truly call his friend. An old friend at that. Doctor Phaleg had brought her to him so many years ago to help him with his true purpose. Nearly twenty six years back.

He did once have another old friend, he remembered. His first real, true friend back when he was just a kid. His friend's name was Derik Poe. After moving from above the deli five years after his father's death, his mom moved them halfway across the planet to the Cinder district in the city of Necros. He and Derik would walk home together from school. Their mothers worked together. They both had lived in small apartments about five blocks from the school. It was the same building, same floor, and their apartments were nearly across the hall from one another. They naturally became best friends.

"Hey kid," he heard a voice. It was coming from a nearby building, where a set of brick stairs led down several feet to the basement of the building. It was cold, so the man wore a cap on his head with only a ponytail of hair being revealed down his back.

Thermonte had stopped and looked. "Me?" he asked, pointing to himself.

The man nodded. "Yea you," he said. "You want to make some money?"

Thermonte thought that was a stupid question. Of course he wanted to make some money. He and his mom could use a little extra. "What do I have to do?"

Derik whispered in his friend's ear. "We gotta get home."

"Our moms will never know," he whispered back to him.

The man in the cap pulled a bulky envelope out from under his coat and handed it to him. "Do you know where Strutter Street is?"

Thermonte nodded that he did. He had always been good with knowing his surroundings. It was back in the direction they had just come.

The man continued, "Go to 364 South Strutter Street, knock on the door and ask for a man called Shade."

Thermonte nodded. He understood everything. "Okay," he said.

"Give this package to him. Tell him Khanel sent you. He will pay you. If he doesn't come see me down here."

Thermonte nodded again and left. The man calling himself Khanel made his way back into the basement door.

As Derik followed his friend, he stopped him. "I think those are bad guys," he said, not knowing how to describe them. He wasn't sure who they were, but he had seen things around the neighborhood.

"If you don't want to go, then go wait for me at our building. Our moms won't be home for several hours. If I can help my mom make some extra money to help her, I will."

Derik had walked a block with him, but then he had

chickened out. He told Thermonte he would meet him back home and ran off in the opposite direction. Thermonte just continued on his way to do his job.

It took him almost twenty minutes to reach the storefront on Strutter Street. It was a jewelry shop of a sort, called Strange Gems, and it looked like it catered to the older kids. The door was locked, so Thermonte rang the bell that was provided.

A man came to the door, dressed in a fine business suit of black and silver. "Yes?" He looked down and saw the fourteen-year-old looking back up at him. "And how may I help such a young one?"

The man was tall and slender. He looked like a giant from young Thermonte's eyes. It took a moment for him to speak. "Um, Khanel sent me."

"Who you here to see?"

"Someone called Shade."

The man opened the door wider and ushered Thermonte inside. "Follow me," he said after closing the door, and made his way across the store and into the back, then down a hallway. The man knocked on the door on the end.

"Yea!" came a muffled shout from behind the door.

The man smiled at Thermonte. Then to the voice, he said, "Khanel sent a boy to see you."

After a very short pause, the man told him to send him in.

Thermonte walked in, still holding the package. "Are you Shade, sir?"

The man behind the desk looked up at the tall man and smiled. "Yea kid, I'm Shade."

Shade had a good tan from the sun, and short black hair sticking up a little from the top of his head. There was a small tattoo on his chin, or was that hair? Thermonte couldn't tell. He handed the package to Shade and said, "Khanel told me you would pay me for this."

Shade waved for him to hand him the envelope, and Thermonte handed it to him. He knew the other guy would pay him if this one did not. Shade opened the package and took a peek inside. Then he looked at the slender man and nodded at him.

The slender man walked over to a small, opened safe, grabbed something, and walked over to stand beside Thermonte, handing it to him. The boy took it. It was fifty talents in coin. He had gotten paid, and very well, too. Thermonte knew his mom only made about two hundred talents in a week cleaning.

Shade smiled at the boy. "You can go now, son. Now go home."

With that, the slender man led him back across the jewelery store and out the door. With the money in his pocket, he walked home and found his friend waiting on the front stoop.

What had happened to his friend Derik? Thermonte thought hard and then he remembered. As he was making something of himself within the Corlesh Clan, Derik stayed behind on Chotis to look after his mother. Derik had known of his plan to bring down the Corlesh Clan for killing his father, and had betrayed him.

He slowly climbed back out of his bed and walked out onto his private balcony, looking out into the sky above. Beyond the city lights trying to mask the sky was cold dark space. That is where he had his old friend killed. He wondered if Derik was still floating out there after all these years.

The door opened up again, and in walked Saffron. Outside the port window, Jon could see a portion of the planet. "We're taking the Chimera down into home base. We will hide it down there and go over it with a fine-toothed comb, so to speak. This ship is far too well known right now. We just heard the Imperium found the FTL and are looking for the yacht now."

"We understand," replied Nicolea and they all followed her to the Chimera.

The Chimera departed from the Condor, piloted by a Union pilot, and headed down to the surface of the planet. Once they entered the world's atmosphere, all they saw was sand and dust. Soon they saw a cliff wall ahead holding a secret docking bay, which was revealed as they came closer. Before long, they were landing inside the mountain.

As they all walked off the Chimera, they were actually met by Grand Admiral Boone. Following close behind him was ex-President Norris, now serving as an adviser. Even though they seemed to be on the side of rebellion, they still had a comforting structure Jon was used to.

After everyone shook hands and was introduced to the Grand Admiral, Norris came up and reunited with his friend. "It is good to see you," he told Jon. "And you still look the same."

"You don't look so bad yourself, sir."

Norris smiled a friendly, relaxing smile. "I'm older, and I show it. But I am good and as healthy as I can be. You know, none of this would be possible without Shepherd's foreknowledge of this. I don't know how he knew."

Nicolea knew how Shepherd knew this was going to happen. He had been reading the books Lenok had with him in his satchel, and knew just who Shepherd really was. That would be a whole new tale. Now, however, was not the time to reveal it.

"Grand Admiral Shepherd was a great man," agreed Boone. "It is because of him we now have this Union of Light. According to him, this is not about just the physical evil of men wanting to take over, but of a spiritual realm, shadows you might say, destroying man from within. It just tells us, there are hidden elements we are not seeing."

By then they were moving out of the docking bay and into the base itself. The base not only held Union military personnel, but families of those that had escaped when the Imperium was formed. Recruiting for the Union was easy in the beginning, but became harder as the empire tightened its grip.

On their way to the debriefing room, they passed military training gyms, barracks, and family housing. The base was huge. They passed family recreation centers and gardens of vegetables and fruits growing under artificial light. All of this was under a mountain covered with thick vegetation on the outside. Only the elite knew that this was an artificial mountain, with an outer covering that was natural.

They learned all of this during their debriefing with

Grand Admiral Solomon Boone, Saffron Baye, and a man they introduced as General Sam Long. General Long was second-in-command to General Brande, who was now an Imperial prisoner. These were the higher ranking officers of the Union of Light. Jon and Nicolea told them everything about their trip and what had happened on the shadow world of Khair Din. It was somewhat confusing at times, and many questions were asked about what happened on the world itself. Many hours later, they were all satisfied with it.

After the debriefing, Nicolea asked Boone about Lamet. Boone called in one of his assistants to take him to see Lamet, who now held a small apartment in the civilian housing district. As Nicolea left them, followed by Soshiana, Saffron headed back to the Condor. It was one of the few battleships they had, and she had to make sure it was not found by the Empire around this world. She needed to make her rounds and she promised she would be back soon.

The base on the world of Dust was considerably larger than anyone would have thought. It was like having an entire city underground, within the giant mountain. It took Nicolea about fifteen minutes to reach his friend. Arnold Lamet, the former Prime

Minister of the Federation, was now confined to a hover-chair permanently. He was in good spirits and was extremely happy when he saw Nicolea walk in.

"Ahh, Nic," smiled Lamet, taking Nicolea's hand.

Nicolea noticed just how feeble the former prime minister had become. His own hand now engulfed his friend's smaller, weaker hand. He wished then that he would have stayed behind, but deep down he knew he had needed to go.

"So what is this getup you're wearing?" Lamet gestured at his clothing.

"I have been to Illosha and I have met the Prophet Warrior from the Book," Nicolea told him, and he saw Lamet smile again.

Lamet said, "You've always been a spiritual man, my friend. You've been passed the mantle."

"He died on that world, but I think he knew I would pick up where he left off." Nicolea was referring to Lenok, who had fought Pan, and died on the shadow world. Both men knew who he was, because both had been followers of the Light. They had even gone to the same church on Deveron.

"And your next step?" Lamet asked.

"I need training and knowledge," Nicolea replied. "I

need to get back to Illosha."

"Easier said than done, my friend."

Nicolea shook his head. "I know, they told us. It's the most guarded planet in the Empire."

"It is man's home world, the beginning of us all. But you need to find a way to get there."

"The Lord will show me a way." Nicolea replied. "Would you like to have lunch? I will let you meet my new friend."

"New friend?"

"Her name is Soshiana, and she has become a newly converted follower of the Light."

Arnold Lamet sat back in his chair. "It would be an honor." As they left, he asked Nicolea, "You still working with the man, Jon Vega, the Agent from the Republic?"

CHAPTER SIX
Call For Help

It took Jon several months to get into the swing of things at the Dust base. Nicolea was filling in as the temporary spiritual leader of the Union. Soshiana was helping Nicolea with his duties and learning more about the Light and her personal past and her future growth. As they were being integrated into the Union of Light, the battleship Condor had been roaming certain sectors of space. They were monitoring the outer systems when a small shuttlecraft entered their proximity.

Admiral Saffron Baye had been called to the bridge immediately. "What is going on?" she asked.

"I'm not sure," reported her second-in-command, Sal Ganat. He was a young man eager to prove himself to the admiral. "It's almost like they are sending out an S.O.S. alert and they seem to be speaking confusing gibberish. I don't think they know how to use a radio comm."

She motioned to the comm tech. "Interrupt their communications and let me speak to them." A moment later, Saffron began to speak. "This is the battleship Condor of the Union of Light Navy. I am Admiral Baye, how may we be of assistance?"

"Praise the Lord of Light," they heard the sigh of one of the occupants of the small shuttle. "My name is Shye Bona, from the world of Sulia on the outskirts of the Empire. We need your help."

"Who is we?"

"We are the Ghel people of Sulia, from the city of Gal-Ganeed. We escaped in this shuttle to find help for our people. We were send to find the Union of Light. Please help us."

Saffron thought for a moment. Then she said, "Scan the shuttle, and bring them aboard. Then bring whoever is on board to interrogation. Then head back to Dust." Before she walked out, she told Sal, "Don't send a message to command, until you hear from me. Just in case this is a trap. Oh, and scan them when they come onto my ship."

"Aye, ma'am," he replied, and gave the order.

After twelve years in space, most of it spent sleeping, Jon felt he needed to be retrained in different areas of his former job. He was training with Ben Gettel. Jon remembered him being a younger man than himself, but he now looked similar in age to Jon. They were in one of the many training gyms working on their hand-to-hand combat technique.

Ben Gettel had been promoted to lieutenant commander in command of ground force troopers under General Brande. But with Brande being in the Black Star prison, and no ships available to transport troops where needed, Ben currently had to just help train those who wished to join and serve the Union.

After the Imperium had risen to power, there were those who continued to join, many working on the outside of the Union sending information when they could. This was also something Ben did to help. General Sam Long would send him on missions to go and gather the information once it had been verified that someone had something for them.

Jon had asked about doing this work, knowing he would have to work under his old, younger friend. He didn't mind, he had always liked Ben. He was beginning to understand how the Lord of Light had been working in his own life. He knew that, perhaps, he was the way he was now because the Lord of Light had plans for him in the future. What it was, he didn't know. But he was beginning to have faith. He had even grabbed himself a copy of the Book Of Light, and read it every morning after he had gotten up. He knew everything in it was the truth. Reading and studying this book every morning had seemed to help him during the day.

Jon Vega did have access to many other things within the Union hierarchy, mainly because of his previous work and who he was. He had always been a trusted Agent in the past, and was still seen as such. When the call came for Ben to go to one of the command interrogations, Jon was allowed to follow and participate. Saffron had brought in the two people she had picked up on the shuttlecraft.

The two people from the world of Sulia sat among the Union personnel, asking for help. Their names were Shye Bona and Juku Chin. Once the room was quiet, Solomon gave the word for the two Ghels to tell their story in a more organized fashion.

Shye started to talk. "The Imperial Planetary Governor, Count Farran, was once a great man, great leader. He treated everyone fairly, regardless of their belief and status in the city. Then when the Empire began creating their new Galactic Constitution, our people suddenly became the lowest end of the pile. Governor Farran immediately banned the worship of Iosa, Lord of the Light, unless we called the Pagonic ruler the Light. If they caught us, we were imprisoned. If you openly defied the ruling, you were killed, or you simply disappeared. Our people, the Ghel, are looked down upon and watched closely. Even by the people and friends we once trusted. They no longer trust us, because they know whom we worship and wait to prove it. People get paid and rewarded for that kind of proof."

"There is the Missionary," Juku spoke then.

"Who is this Missionary?" Grand Admiral Boone asked. Standing behind him was Admiral Baye, and next to her was General Long.

It was Juku who told about the Missionary. "We don't know his true name, he is only known as the Missionary. Governor Farran has been looking for him for a long time, but cannot find him, and no one is talking. Not any of our people at any rate. He is the one that got me and Shye off-world to search for you. This was his plan,"

"God's plan," Shye corrected.

"Oh yes, God's plan," Juku continued. "Anyway, I think he is hoping to find someone he calls the Prophet Warrior."

Jon took a glance at Nicolea, who just smiled back. Without any training he already seemed to have a job. "So what is the rest of this Missionary's plan?" Jon asked.

"He wants us to bring someone back with us to Sulia. There he can show you the rest of the plan to help us escape and get to Ephesus," Shye replied. "We don't even know the full plan yet."

"And you trust this man, do you?" asked Solomon.

Both of the visitors nodded and agreed that they did. After a few more questions, Admiral Boone led the way out of the room, and stood to talk to the others.

"I'm not too sure about this," he commented to his team. "It could be a trap, and in fact it sounds like an obvious trap."

"I don't think it is," Nicolea replied. "If they had not brought up the Missionary, I too would be apprehensive."

"Who is this Missionary?" Solomon asked him.

Nicolea stepped forward. "His full title is the

Missionary of Light, and he is sent to lead the Ghel people from slavery and other persecution. He has also been used to eradicate total depravity from cities and the like."

"So if this is a real situation, why does this Missionary need help?"

Nicolea answered him. "We don't all live on a single world anymore. Mankind has expanded into the stars, and has more than tripled ninety times over. Mankind is now uncountable and things are different than they were in ancient times."

"Still," Solomon said, "We need to be cautious."

Jon came forward. "I'll go with him," he said. "If we can survive twelve years in deep space, I'll see to it we survive this, if it is a trap. Personally, I would trust anything Nicolea says about any situation."

Grand Admiral Boone thought deep and hard on this, but agreed to it. "How many can fit into the shuttle, besides the two guests?"

"It looked to be a six-man shuttle," Saffron told them.

"And do the two guests know where we are now?"

"No, sir," Saffron again replied. "No details were ever given to them."

"Okay, Nicolea and Jon are in charge of this mission." Boone stated. "Take Gettel with you, Jon. Consider it more training." Then he turned to Nicolea and said, "Take your friend Soshiana with you. She seems to be able to handle almost anything."

Nicolea nodded. "She would probably insist anyway," he smiled.

Solomon laid out his own plan to get to Sulia. "Admiral Baye, you will take them to the spot you picked them up at, and let them go from there. Stay there until you hear from our team. If you have to leave, don't be gone for long. Also, if you find it to be a trap, leave immediately."

"Yes, sir."

"Everyone report back as soon as we know anything." Everyone agreed, and the next morning they were all on board the Condor, heading out to their previous rendezvous.

They had been on the shuttle for two days before the world of Sulia appeared in front of them. As the world came closer, Shye, who was flying the shuttle, activated a pre-planned navigational control which would take them automatically to a specific location. Once it was activated, Shye turned toward the others.

"We will land outside of Gal-Ganeed in the thick forest hills of Onstringe," Shye told them. "The Missionary will meet us there and guide us into the hills and under into the city without being seen."

"We'll have to move fast, just in case Count Farran's troops decide to head out to our landing location," Juku added.

"Are we sure the Missionary will meet us?" Ben asked. He had been quiet through this mission so far, talking only to Jon and Nicolea. He held his weapon close, for he had Solomon Boone's hesitancy.

"He promised," Juku nodded.

Nicolea smiled. "It will be fine. This has all happened before."

Thermonte wandered alone in the palace on Bel Terra, remembering his past. It was what he usually did now, at least when the palace hallways seemed to be empty. He had a suspicion that things were taking place, and he felt he needed to know about them, him being the emperor. He remembered asking Doctor Phaleg what he was a doctor of, and Phaleg gave him that grin. "I am no doctor, but people tend to trust those with the title."

He remembered the first thing he ever did for Phaleg. It was the first of many.

Leon and Banko, who had been two of his most trusted men, brought Gedor, the shameful admiral of the Federation, into the office. Thermonte had been sitting down behind his desk and got to work.

"I need to make that deal." *Gedor was feeling anxious. He had been on the run and hiding since the war ended three weeks ago.*

"And what deal was that?" Thermonte asked.

"I want to work for this friend you have."

Thermonte thought for a moment. "Maybe I should just turn you in to the Republic, or better yet, perhaps the Federation will pay more."

Gedor moaned.

Thermonte laughed. "It will take about a week to get a transport here to pick you up." To Leon, he said, "Take him to the apartment next to the docking bay, and don't let him out. I don't want to see him until he leaves."

"You got it, boss," replied Leon, grabbing Gedor by his arm, and moving him toward the hidden doorway behind the desk.

Thermonte smiled as he remembered Admiral Gedor begging for his help. Being in charge was very good. Then he remembered what an arrogant man

Gedor had been when they had first met. They had first met on the Ofidian space station; Admiral Gedor and two of his officers had been escorted to Thermonte's office. Gedor looked to be a proud man. He wasn't very tall, but the way he walked, he projected that he was taller than he was. After the first few moments of speaking, Thermonte realized that Gedor thought himself to be someone of great importance.

The first thing out of Gedor's mouth as he was walking into the office was, "I won't take anything off of anyone." He was loud and sounded sure of himself.

"So what makes you think I'm here to take anything from you?" Thermonte shot back.

That made Gedor angry, and when his men put their hands on the pistols hanging in their holsters, Thermonte's men already had their weapons out and pointed at their heads. The godfather then said, "Maybe we should all just calm down, Admiral."

Gedor thought about it for a moment, then agreed, relaxing himself slowly. "So what am I doing here, and not out there blowing away this space station?"

"There are too many innocent people on this station, so why would you blow it up?"

Gedor just smiled, and in his arrogance, he said, "It will not intimidate me at all. No one is innocent, and if they are here when I strike, then they go down with the station. I started this Borders War, and no one is the wiser. Both sides blame each other. So I will easily take down this station with no problem. My men are loyal to me, so no one will care."

Thermonte leaned back in his chair. "So tell me, Admiral, what can we do to not have you destroy this station?"

"The House of Taran wants this station," Gedor told him straight out. "Of course they will share with you. They get seventy. You get thirty."

"I took this station from the Corlesh Clan myself. I get eighty and the House gets twenty."

Gedor smiled. "I don't think so. The House of Taran has many more resources than your little Electrik Syndicate does. The House gets control."

Seeing how quick the pride came out in this man, Thermonte thought it was about time to dangle the deal. "How would you like to take control of your own fleet, or should I say your own armada?"

"Are you saying you have an armada hidden somewhere?"

"Let's just say I have access to one," replied Thermonte. "The job is yours if you want it."

It appealed to Gedor, and Thermonte knew it. "What do I have to do to get my own armada?"

"Nothing."

Then one of Gedor's men heard something in his ear, which held a military grade earpiece. He then leaned in and tapped Gedor on the shoulder. "Sir, there are Republic battleships moving toward our sector. We need to get back now, sir."

Frustrated, Gedor stood up. "We'll take this up later, Mister Electrik. I got to get back."

This told Thermonte that Admiral Gedor did have those above him he had to listen to. "Tell you what, you fight your war, and when you want to make a deal, just come see me at my home on Chotis. Leon here will see you there with no trouble, and no harm will come to you."

"We'll see," was the last thing Thermonte heard from Gedor as he moved out quickly, heading for his shuttlecraft.

Thermonte watched him go. Then he turned toward Leon. "Once we leave, get everyone off the station, and move this thing to our hiding place," he said. "Then you guys get back to Chotis. We're shutting this thing down for a short time."

"Will do, boss."

Thinking back on these things, Thermonte wished he had more to do around here. He wondered if he could create something. Perhaps he could come up with a mission for Bjorn to do, or that Andrelus fellow. Now that he thought about it, Thermonte realized he didn't even know where Andrelus was at the moment.

CHAPTER SEVEN

Utopian Shipyards

As the shuttle was touching down in a small clearing in Onstringe, they could see a man stepping out from the forest in modern clothing, watching. It was the Missionary, according to Juku. After landing, they all walked out of the shuttle and followed the Missionary back into the thick forest.

The Missionary himself wasn't particularly tall, but of average height. He had a graying beard, trimmed short to match his hair.

As they walked, the forest became more dense, then there was a small cave entrance. They entered the cave, and after several feet of being in near darkness, the corridor from the entrance opened up into a larger cavern, lit by torches of fire lined up around the wall. On the far side, the cavern went even deeper.

But it was here that the Missionary stopped and

turned and offered his thanks. He looked at Nicolea curiously. "You're a Ghel, are you not?"

Jon looked at his friend, who nodded toward the Missionary. Nicolea said, "From the tribe of Dan."

The Missionary smiled. "The lost tribe finally finds their way home. You are the Prophet Warrior, yes?"

"I am."

"Another prophecy, soon to be fulfilled," the Missionary said, and gave him a hug. "Just goes to prove just how amazing the Lord is."

Then to Juku, he said, "Your wife is asking for you. She is preparing food for us all. During the meal, I will tell you what we must do," he told the rest. "But we have to act quickly."

It took them about an hour to make it beneath the city of Gal-Ganeed, and then up into the streets. They were moving ever so slowly. Pagonic troops were out in sets of two or three, walking the streets, looking for those not operating within their laws. Pagonic laws were binding within all of the galaxy, and most of those laws had nothing to do with morality, but were strictly enforced. The level of enforcement, and punishment, was at the discretion of the planetary governor.

The troopers knew most of the people of the city by

their faces. Newcomers were always stopped and asked for paperwork. Jon, Nicolea, Soshiana, and Ben did not have papers of any kind, so they needed to be cautious in making their way to Juku's home.

Gal-Ganeed was built upon the underground ruins of the ancient city of Gal-Ganeed, which is how the Missionary got around without being seen. The Pagonic troops and government knew nothing of the ruins, since most of the documents and paperwork for the ancient city had been lost long ago. Entrances into the ancient city were actually located all around the newer city. Many of the entrances were leading into the city sewage, but below that led to the underground city. The Missionary led them up one of these sewer entrances, slid open the grate, then led them quietly down the street.

Light was dimming and they knew they had to move fast because of the curfew imposed at sunset. When darkness came, so did the troopers in excess on the streets. There were a few robotic drones flying around the streets to help, so they had to try and avoid them as well, and soon they were in Juku's home. With dinner served, they began to talk.

"So just what kind of help do you need from the

Union?" Jon asked him.

"You need to get these people out of the city and get them off-world," replied the Missionary, "and you need to get them to the Ephesus."

"Where is this, Ephesus?"

The Missionary smiled. "What is Ephesus," he corrected. "The Ephesus is an exodus ship, designed to take the Ghel to a safe and new world."

Jon looked back at his friends, then returned his gaze to the Missionary. "Just how many people are we talking here?"

"Around five hundred."

Jon leaned back in his chair. "Just how are we going to achieve this?"

"Trust in Iosa, His Light will lead the way, my friend." The Missionary continued to smile, pausing for only a moment. "There is a plan in place."

Nicolea, who was sitting next to Jon, placed his hand on Jon's shoulder, fearing he would become angry. But Jon remained calm. He was little bit frustrated, but nothing more. To the Missionary, Nicolea asked, "Just what is this plan?"

The Missionary immediately began to speak. He spoke to Nicolea. "You and the young lady will help get these people away from the city. There will be a distraction when the time comes, so you will have to move very quickly." Then, to Jon, he said, "You and your partner," he indicated Ben sitting on the other side of Jon, "will head out to the Utopian shipyards and bring back the ships to pick up the people and escort them to Ephesus."

"But we've never heard of the Utopian shipyards," Ben answered. "I mean, who runs it?"

"The operator of the shipyards could probably tell you more, but it began secretly by followers of the Light, all who worked for the Ikon shipyards," the Missionary told them. "I believe the man you knew as Shepherd helped to set it up when he was younger. Before he became a Grand Admiral."

"And you have these coordinates?" Jon asked him.

"I do, and I will write them down for you, before you leave in the morning."

"That soon?" Jon asked him.

"Time is everything," the Missionary told them. "It will take time to get everything together. We need to get the Ghel to the rendezvous, and it will also take time for you, Jon, to get together the Spearhead ships and return to gather the Ghel."

"Spearhead ships?"

The Missionary just smiled. "That is what Shepherd named them. They were specifically built for the Union, though some are constructed for the escort for the Ephesus to the new world, far from here."

After a another moment of silence, Jon leaned back in his chair again. After hearing the messages and words of his friend Nicolea on the journey home from Khair Din, he had become closer to accepting the Lord of Light into his life, and living the marvels of salvation. He was also finding things out about his old friends that he had never known. "You knew Admiral Shepherd?" he asked the Missionary point-blank.

"I met him one time, and he knew who I was." The Missionary locked eyes on Jon's. "I met him on Illosha, and we spoke about this very moment, which we both knew was to come."

Jon had been to Illosha, and thoughts of it still confused him a bit. It was a different place in space and time it seemed, according to the way he perceived it. Illosha was a very different place. "Are we going to get through this?" he asked the Missionary.

"That is up to you, Jon," he answered him.

With that, dinner was over. Jon and Ben prepared to

leave in the morning, and Soshiana and Nicolea discussed the preparations for the departure of the Ghel from the city. According to the Missionary, the entire populace of the Ghel already knew the timeline, when they had to meet in the ancient city below.

Early that next morning, the Missionary led Jon and Ben back to another shuttle that was hidden away from the Pagonic troops. Nicolea accompanied them, to see them off. On his way to the shuttle, Nicolea had leaned in to Jon and said, "Have faith and trust, my friend. It will all work out in the end. Follow the Light."

Jon had always found Nicolea's knowledge of the Faith of the Light impressive. Knowing he had once been a government officer much like himself, he found it amazing he had that much faith. Soon he and Ben had boarded the shuttle and lifted off.

Two days later, they were back on board the Condor, and were telling Saffron what had transpired. "I'm sending a message to the Stormbringer," she said, "and I'm going to ask Astarte to join us."

"Malcolm Astarte?" Jon asked her.

She nodded as they walked down the corridor. "Yep. He is next in line for a promotion to admiral, you might say. He would have been promoted already, but we only have the two battleships."

"So you're over him?"

"Officially yes, but we are the same, and with the present situation, we both just listen to Boone," she answered. "He is the real genius. He'll want to come also."

Jon stopped her. "Are you going to Dust first? That's not in the time-line, and we don't have time for that."

She looked a bit irritated at him. "He'll meet us partway." Then she stared at him concernedly. "You do have the coordinates, don't you?"

"Of course I do."

"Then come on," she waved her hand for him to follow, as she started to walk again. "Lets go to navigation, then I'll send the communications." The thought of actually getting more ships for the Union felt exciting. It could turn the tide in the war.

Once on the bridge, Jon gave up the coordinates of the shipyards given to him by the Missionary. The location was a surprise. They would have to head deeper into the inner worlds of the Empire, around the uninhabitable world of Nod. Nod was a large gaseous world located just within the Dinhabah system. Jon had been told to look just within Nod's outer atmosphere. This location had helped to keep the shipyards from being found yet.

Malcolm Astarte responded in another coded communication saying he would meet them there. Solomon Boone would take one of the long-range shuttles and meet them in the Dothe System. It was an almost halfway point. When the Grand Admiral arrived, he had more transport shuttles with him.

When all four of the shuttles were docked in the battleship's main docking bay, Jon and Saffron realized that the shuttles carried skeletal bridge crews. Saffron saluted Boone loosely when he walked up and said, "As always, you're thinking ahead."

"This is exciting news, if it's true," Solomon replied. "This would put us on even ground with the Empire." As they walked toward the bridge, he said, "I was amazed Shepherd had all this set up when the time came. He was decades before his time."

"Grand Admiral Shepherd was a great man," she agreed. "And a great leader."

Behind them, Jon added, "He was also a great friend."

Solomon stopped then, and turned to look at him. "Amen, brother," he said, placing a hand on Jon's shoulder. "That he was." They both smiled, then Solomon turned and started walking again. "Let's go take care of this and not let Shepherd down."

The light from the Dinhaban sun gave the world of Nod a violet color of swirling gas. At some point in time, a probe had been sent to survey Nod. The gases in the lower atmosphere had dissolved the probe before it could reach the bottom, and no further probes had been sent.

When the Condor reached their destination, they found the Stormbringer already waiting. Jon recognized Astarte's voice. "You've gotten slow, Admiral."

He thought he was speaking to Saffron, but it was Solomon who replied in the same manner. "Don't you mean Grand Admiral?"

"Always good to have the boss here, sir," was Astarte's reply.

"So have you located the shipyards yet?"

"Well, sir," Malcolm answered, "we found the fleet of about thirty large battleships just below the atmosphere, but have no way to get to them. We found the actual shipyards behind the black moon of the planet. We all thought it was a dead moon, but it seems to be inhabited."

"What?" Solomon was surprised, as was everyone.

"No worries, sir, those working within the Utopian shipyards tell me they are a friend of the Union. The giant ship they have constructed there in the shipyards is incredible. They call it an Exodus-class ship."

"Okay, you and Admiral Baye stay on your ships in case we have company. I will take Jon and Ben and we'll take a shuttle and go talk to the shipyards' administrator."

A little bit after that, Solomon, Jon, and Ben were in a shuttle heading behind the black moon of Nod. Over the horizon of the back of the moon, what they saw was amazing. It surely wasn't as big as the Ikon shipyards, but it was just as impressive. Visually, if a ship passed, they would have never seen it. The effects of the gas of Nod and the elements of the moon hid the shipyards from radar scanners. Solomon was impressed with just how long they had stayed hidden from the Empire, or from anyone for that matter. But, of course, Grand Admiral Shepherd had been involved.

They had brought several armed Union soldiers for

protection, but it soon was apparent that they had been unnecessary. The soldiers stayed behind on the shuttle with the pilots.

The administrator of the Utopian shipyards was named Nate Polaris. He was an older man, and had been there when Shepherd had set up the plan. He led them throughout the facility and showed them the Ephesus. It was a truly monumental ship. It would hold at least ten thousand people, if necessary. It would have seemed like an excessive amount of space for the five hundred Ghels on Sulia, but everyone knew that there was a reason for everything Shepherd had done.

The Ephesus was divided into three main tubular sections. These main sections were the biosphere sections, where life would be lived. These large tubes were connected by a smaller tube running the length of the entire ship. This tube contained a transport train between the sections. Around the transport tube, four smaller tubes connected one section to another, and could be used as simple walkways between the sections.

On the rear of the ship was an extra portion which seemed to blossom out like a flower. This portion contained the engines that would propel the ship to its unknown destination. On the front of the giant ship was another extra portion which contained the small flight bridge of the Exodus-class ship. The front of the bridge protruded out in a double nylon glass dome to allow for an impressive view of the stars.

A wide variety of vegetation grew on the deep layer of soil that covered the inner hull of the biosphere sections. Between the inner and outer hulls much of the structure for the various ship's systems had been hidden away. This area was readily, but unobtrusively, accessible for maintenance and repairs.

Around the outer hull were seven docking points at which other starships could connect and access the Ephesus. Two docking points were located on each of the biosphere sections. The lead section had a docking point where a ship could connect to the top, just above the bridge of the Ephesus. The Spearhead escort ships would connect to the docking points on the biosphere sections.

Soon after the tour, they sat down to talk. Nate was telling them about the six Spearhead ships that would go with the Ephesus as guardians of the journey ahead, when Solomon received an alert from Admiral Baye. "Go ahead."

"We have two Pagonic dreadnoughts heading our

way. They must have seen our battleships, what do we do?"

Turning to Nate, Solomon asked, "How do we get to the ships in the planet's atmosphere?"

"Send shuttles down, I suppose," Nate replied to him. "The upper atmosphere just masks the ships' signatures. It's not dangerous."

Then back to Saffron Solomon said, "Send those bridge crews to the ships below by shuttlecraft, get them started and take out the dreadnoughts. Don't let them send our location to anyone else."

"Are there any special instructions we need to start the new ships?" Saffron asked, speaking for one of the captains.

Nate quickly responded to her himself. "They're ready to go. It operates much like the old standard Ikon battleships. Just don't go over half power or fire weapons until you are out of the atmosphere."

"You catch that?" Solomon asked her.

"We got it."

"They've started their attack." That was Astarte. "We need to protect the shuttles."

As soon as the fight began, Jon and Ben headed back to the shuttle. As quickly as they could, they lifted off and began to follow the others into the planet's atmosphere. Grand Admiral Boone stayed behind. He would be able to rejoin Saffron once the battle was over.

Fighters from the Pagonic dreadnoughts swarmed out from the bowels of their ships like a plaque of locusts. They were met by the few Ikon fighters the two battleships had left. They clashed in the light of explosions and the energy blasts that came from the fighters. The shuttles soon reached the atmosphere of the planet. In the fogginess of the upper atmosphere, they came across the first six Spearhead ships sitting there waiting to be boarded. The five shuttles carrying the crews split from their formation and each headed to a separate ship. Jon and Ben headed to the sixth Spearhead.

They left the shuttle in the docking bay and made their way as fast as they could to the bridge of the ship. As they made their way to the bridge, glowing blue lights automatically came on just before them. The bridge completely lit up as soon as they stepped onto it. It looked much like a standard Ikon battleship bridge, but then these were essentially Ikon-built ships with slight upgrades. Above the front viewport sat a plaque with the ship's number and name: New Haven, Ephesus

Escort One.

Jon stared at it for a moment, then looked over at Ben. "Seems Shepherd thought of everything, didn't he?" Ben just smiled back, and they watched the skeleton crew start the ship up like they had always been there.

When the communications came online, they heard Astarte's voice coming through. "Are you guys ready yet? We have two more dreadnoughts coming in."

Jon took the communication headset from the officer and put it on his head. "We're on our way."

Calling to the other Spearhead battleships, he said, "Give confirmation ship ID."

"Captain Dozier on the Cora."

"Captain McCord on the Gold Dust."

"Captain Goddin on the Keystone."

"Captain Miller on the Oceana."

"Captain Sousley on the Skylark."

"This is Commander Jon Vega," Jon answered them. "Lets get these Spearheads out of here and take out those other two ships."

All six of the Spearhead ships began to move in unison, heading straight out of the thick atmosphere of the planet. The officer at the main weapons control turned and looked at Jon. "There are four light rail cannons at the very front of these ships, loaded and ready to fire."

Ben looked over and saw the grin on Jon's face. He knew what he was thinking. Then he heard Jon say, "Head straight for the two newcomers, and lets test out those light rail cannons. Oceana and Keystone, fire at the nearest with me, the others fire at the one behind. Two bursts apiece should do it, but ready a third just in case."

The six Spearhead ships shot out from the planet's atmosphere, immediately firing giant balls of energy from those light rail cannons, a mixture of projectile and weaponized light. The newly arrived Pagonic ships were still releasing their fighters as they were struck by the rail cannon fire. They quickly broke apart and were swallowed up in their own fire.

"You guys go ahead and do what you need to do," came Saffron's voice over the communication speakers. "We'll mop up the mess here. No word of this place will get out." With that, the six Spearhead ships left and headed for the world of Sulia, to the selected coordinates given to them by the Missionary.

CHAPTER EIGHT

Exodus Into The Stars

Nicolea stood with the Missionary as the shuttle carrying his friend Jon lifted up into space to find the Utopian shipyards. Soshiana stood behind them, quietly. Once the shuttle had left the view of those on the ground, the Missionary turned to Nicolea and said, "We should speak before we have to depart. We have about a week before that happens." He peeked over at Soshiana. "I need to speak with you alone."

Nicolea watched the Missionary lead Soshiana back the way they came. He hung back so the other two could talk, but kept them in his sight. Once they reached the cavern entrance into the city's underground, the Missionary was waiting for him. Soshiana had moved on.

"She has gone to help get things ready," the Missionary explained to him. "It will take about a week or so before it is the time to head out." As they walked deeper into the cave, he asked, "You know she's an abomination?"

Nicolea nodded. "I know, and when I first met her, she acted like an abomination, working for Thermonte Electrik, doing that which was evil. And after speaking with her after all these years, I believe she has changed. Once she was stiff, robotic, acting like a bio-tek. But after these years, teaching her, talking to her, we found out that it wasn't her idea to become what she is now. She seems to have a mind of her own now. She has her free will back."

"Does she know that what she is is considered an abomination in the Light?"

"She does," Nicolea answered. "She also knows there is hope for her, and that everything is possible with the Lord of Light. All she has to do is to believe in the life, death, and resurrection of Iosa. I believe she is on the road to the recovery of her soul."

The Missionary smiled. "I pray she is, for every soul is precious."

That evening, Nicolea finally got to spend some time alone. He removed one of the scrolls from his satchel, lit a candle within the cave he was staying in, and read.

Nearby, Soshiana lay near the burning fire. He didn't know if she was sleeping, or if she even could sleep. She seemed to have been doing more and more relaxing since she had been learning about the Lord of Light. He wasn't going to bother her.

He just smiled and commenced reading the scroll.

Gideon came down to see Lenok every night he was in the dungeon. On the third night, after Gideon had left and all was quiet, the White Seraph appeared before the Prophet Warrior and spoke to him.

"The next night when Gideon comes forth to visit with you, you must give him instruction and he will have to follow it to the letter. You must tell Gideon to tell the Ghel people to sacrifice the youngest of their flock and spread its blood above the door of their homes. They are to do this on the eve of the decree coming to fruition. Not before, for the blood will be dried and of no use.

"Then he is to find and take both pieces of your staff, and at the beginning of dusk on that very eve, hold them together where they were broken and pray, asking for the mending of the staff, where he will see a great miracle. Then he will take the staff and confront the Duke, giving him one last chance to release the Ghel people. If he yet refuses to do so, then Gideon must raise the staff above his head, and strike the ground with the top of it. Thus will another great miracle be revealed."

"What of the three soldiers that believe as Gideon do, and have brought me here to this city?" Lenok asked.

The White Seraph answered, saying, "They must do as the Ghel people do, using the same blood as the Ghel are using. Thus, will they and their families be spared. Between the twin lakes, they must spend the time integrating into the Ghel."

So on the fourth night when Gideon came down to check on Lenok, bringing him food, the Prophet Warrior told him what the White Seraph had said. Lenok said, "Go and tell the Ghel people to sacrifice the youngest of their flock and spread its blood above the door of their homes. They are to do this on the eve of the decree coming to fruition. Not before, for the blood will be dried and of no use.

"Also, tell the three men that you trusted to guide me, Stark, Manis, and Kanis, to do as the Ghel people with the same sacrifice and the same blood. Then will they and their families be saved."

Then Gideon asked, "Do I do the same although I have no family?"

Lenok then answered, "You are to find both pieces of my staff that was broken and at the beginning of dusk on the very eve, you are to pray and ask for the mending of the staff, where you will witness that miracle, which will give you much encouragement. Then you will take the staff and confront the Duke, giving him one final chance to release the Ghel people, and *if he refuses, you must raise the staff high, and strike the ground with the top of the staff hard. That will be a second great miracle."*

On the eve of the decree, Stark, Manis, Kanis, and the Ghel people began their sacrifice. Then they marked their doors with the blood of the youngest of the flock as was told to them by Gideon.

Gideon then found the two pieces of Lenok's staff, and when dusk was upon them, Gideon then knelt in prayer holding the two pieces against their broken ends and prayed for the reconstruction of the staff. The staff was restored just as the sun settled beyond the darkness of the night. Taking the staff, he made his way to the throne room where Duke Poden was conversing with the priests of Pan, as was duty at that hour.

"May I have a word with you, Master Duke?" he asked, as they all turned around.

"Speak your mind, Captain," the duke replied.

The priests turned and moved to the side of their duke, to watch and listen to what Gideon had to say. Gideon moved up closer holding the staff of the Prophet Warrior.

"I thought I broke that thing," the duke said, pointing to the staff. "What are you doing with it?"

"Truth is, sir, I am a worshiper of the Lord of the Light, and I am here to give you one last chance to release the people of Ghel from their servitude."

Anger swelled up in the duke, and he stood up, pointing a crooked finger at Gideon. "Kill this traitor."

As soon as the throne room guards moved against Gideon, he raised up the staff of the Prophet Warrior and struck the ground with the head of the staff, just as the White Seraph had instructed. It was then that the second great miracle happened.

A loud noise rang throughout the city, and when it was over, Lenok had been freed from the chains that bound him. The prison had been opened and guards were no longer there.

Lenok followed the stairs up out of the dungeon and made his way to the throne room. There he found his staff lying on the floor as one piece. Everyone was gone, including Gideon. Lenok knew that the White Seraph had taken him. He had been chosen for a purpose.

Lenok picked up his staff and made his way into the city to check on the Ghel people.

A caravan of large air-vehicles was lined up in a giant cave near the coast. Over the last few days the thirty or so vehicles had been filled with possessions and food, and then carefully moved out of the city. Air-buses were left behind to carry the people the two hundred miles to the coast, where they would be met by their rescue team. This caravan would be spotted and draw attention, for they were to leave at dawn.

But there was a plan.

The Missionary would stay behind and draw attention away from the departing caravan of buses. After giving Nicolea and Soshiana their instructions, and speaking to the people, who were now lined up and ready to leave, the Missionary made his way through the streets of Gal-Ganeed towards the home and office of Count Farran.

As the sunlight began to shine over the city, Count Farran opened his eyes. He was still in his nice plush bed in the mountain-top palace from where he governed the city. He noticed something strange about the sunlight. As the light began a bright and beautiful morning, the light itself began to turn a strange tint of red. It didn't bother him at first, but before long it started to aggravate him.

He threw the covers off of himself, and made his way to the large windowed door that led out onto his private balcony. He opened it and walked out. He looked up at the system's sun itself, but the bright red ball of fire kept him from seeing more.

Then it hit him. *A red sun,* he thought to himself. Impossible and strange.

As the spots in his eyes from glaring at the sun began to clear, he noticed a figure standing in the courtyard of the palace. It was the Missionary. It was the man he had been trying to catch and kill all year long.

"Guards!" Farran shouted back into the palace. "Guards!"

Several of the palace guards, all dressed in the Pagaonic uniform, rushed inside to stand before the Count. Farran grabbed the nearest guard and pulled him out onto the balcony and pointed to the Missionary. "Catch that man now!" he shouted in anger into the guard's ear. "Kill him if you have to, but bring me his body dead or alive!"

The guards left quickly, and the count turned to go back in to get dressed, when the Missionary spoke. "You have but one chance to save your people and your city, Count Farran."

Grimacing, the count turned back around toward the man. "And what is that?!"

"Turn back to the Lord of the Light, and remove yourselves from this place." Just as he had said that, several Pagonic soldiers came up beside him, grabbing him.

Count Farran smiled. "I have made my choice,

Missionary," he told him. Then to the soldiers he said, "Bind him between the Horns of Pan. We're going to show him some Pagonic justice today."

The courtyard of the palace was a large circular area, opened to the elements of the mountain top, usually with a cool breeze blowing steadily through. There was no breeze this morning as all the soldiers, guards, and followers of the Pagonic faith gathered to see justice fall to this traitor. Within about half an hour, Count Farran walked out onto the grand platform to preside over the court. The sun was still bright, and still contained the red tint, as everyone could now see.

The Horns of Pan were curved posts coming up from the ground, in the shape of the horns of a goat, only curving out to the sides toward the top. The Missionary's wrists were secured to the posts with chains made from Synoan steel, the strongest steel found. It was so strong, it was used in the construction of their warships.

"Our Pagonic Scribe will now list the charges against this man against the Crown of the Imperium," Count Farran announced to the crowd as a little man with a deep voice walked up to stand next to him.

The scribe spoke, reading the list he had been told to

write down. "This man, known as the Missionary, has been arrested, and the charges brought against him by the people of the Imperium are as follows:

"Inciting the people to riot. Preaching forbidden laws and spreading the false teachings of the ancient God of Light. Treason to the Imperium crown and praying to his false God, being the old God of Light. Being a follower of the ancient prophet Iosa, by saying he is the Son of the Lord of Light." He listed off several more made up charges, and stepped back away from the count to give him the stage.

He said, "How do you plead, Missionary?"

"Last chance, Count."

"Your plea, infidel?"

"By your standards, and the rule of this false governing body, it will probably end up being guilty, regardless of what is said today." He smiled and closed his eyes.

"Then you are sentenced to death by the removal of your head." Then the count motioned for the executioner to step forward.

The Missionary opened his eyes and spoke. "All is as it should be. The Ghel have all left and are safe and my purpose is about to be fulfilled."

This caused the count's eyes to look harder into the crowd. Usually, everyone in the city was present to see the justice of a criminal, but the more he looked, the less people he saw. Before he could speak or cry out, he watched the Missionary break the Synoan chains and pull out a silver rod from somewhere within his sleeve. He shook it once and it extended into a staff.

"My name is Gideon, and the one true God, the Lord of the Light, calls this place a wicked place, and a witch's mountain, and it therefore will be destroyed by His hand."

Guards and soldiers rushed him, but Gideon was too fast. He smote them with the staff and they burned into ash that floated to the ground. At that moment, panic hit everyone there, and Gideon saw the realized fear in Farran's eyes, and he struck the ground with the staff.

In the far distance, traveling on the road, a sound similar to a sonic boom could be heard. Nicolea and Soshiana turned to the mountain that housed the Ghel city, but it was no more. It had collapsed into the forests of Onstringe, which still stood strong.

"Do you think he died, doing what he had to do?" Soshiana asked him.

"I don't know," was Nicolea's reply. "I have a feeling there is more to it than that."

The Ghel had been waiting on the shores of Glass Lake, south of Vann Loth, for two days. Through visual and radar, they had noticed that Vann Loth was sending re-con ships to find out what had happened to the city in the mountains. A mountain that now could not be found.

Nicolea had just finished eating when Juku ran up to him and Soshiana sitting by the water's edge. Juku had been monitoring the communications radio on the channel given to them by the Missionary. "They're here," he said excitedly. "They're asking for you," he said to Nicolea.

Nicolea got up quickly and followed Juku to the radio. "This is Nicolea. Jon, is that you?"

"Yea, we're here and we're coming up on Sulia. We jumped in just within the system, to give you more time."

Nicolea smiled. "We've been ready for two days, my friend." Then he saw something from the direction of the city. Squadrons of Harbinger fighters were lifting up from within the city's hanger bays and heading out into the open space above. "You're about to have company from below ya," he relayed to Jon. "Hope you got some sort of defense."

"You should see these bad boys we just acquired," Jon answered. "They throw a mean punch." Nicolea smiled, he knew what that meant. Jon continued, "Get ready for the shuttles, we are about to send them down."

With the help of Juku and his wife, and Shye and her friends, they prepared for the Ghel departure from Sulia.

As a small battle was taking place just above the planet, the shuttles began to land and the Ghel people lined up according to their old tribe names. The shuttles had to land many times to bring the entire group up, and the whole process took about seven hours.

The small fleet of Spearhead battleships picked off the Harbinger fighters one by one. It wasn't too long before three large Pagonic battleships appeared from around one of the moons of Sulia. They launched their fighters, and that is when the Union launched their new fighters. The battle was quickly over, and the Pagonic ships destroyed.

Jon's crew had been able to jam communications, so no other Pagonic ships could be notified. After the initial fight, the rest of the exodus from Sulia was extremely easy. When ground troops eventually arrived to investigate the area, all they found were deserted vehicles and some trash that was blowing around in the wind.

Once the last of the shuttles had made it back safely, the small Union fleet of Spearheads jumped immediately, heading straight back to the Utopian shipyards.

Several months had passed, and the Union had started activating many of the Spearhead ships at the newly acquired shipyards. The original six had been specifically constructed to connect to the Ephesus to go with it on the long journey that it was being prepped to take. The Ephesus and its escort ships would be leaving in another two or three months.

Grand Admiral Solomon Boone was walking back to his quarters on the Dust base, when his brother stopped him. "Abagael and I are going to take Maggie and head out with the Ephesus."

"You will be missed," Solomon replied. "We just met back up, and it was nice being a family for a little while." He would miss them. At least he had gotten another chance to be with family for a time.

"I moved to Dust to get away from this war, only to involve us in the war again. I want to keep my family as safe as I can."

Solomon nodded. "Trust me, I understand. I wish you the best, little brother. You keep your family safe, and at least perhaps the Boone name will live on."

Jesse smiled and came in to give his older brother a hug. "You be careful out there fighting this war."

Solomon then handed him a coded folding device he had just pulled out of his pocket. "Carry this with you and plug it into one of the communication screens on the Ephesus," he said. "We should be able to speak to one another for at least several years. That big ship isn't going to go that fast. The code and number for me is already set up for it. I had a feeling you might consider going."

"We will. Love you, brother."

"Love you, too," Solomon replied. "You take care of that perfect family of yours."

About two months later, the Cora, the Gold Dust, the Keystone, the Oceana, the Skylark, and the New Haven had all connected to the Ephesus and were preparing to go. All of their original captains had volunteered to go with them. Jon had now been assigned to the Spearhead ship Republic. He was on board, on his way to meet with Grand Admiral Solomon Boone, when he ran into his friend Saffron Baye. She now had additional bars added to her jacket, denoting the rank of grand admiral.

"Grand admiral, I see," Jon greeted her. "Congratulations."

"Yea, Solomon just promoted me," she told him. "You know I'm leaving with the Ephesus when they go? That will be my new fleet."

Jon was taken aback a bit, but then he thought about it. He had always figured that he and Saffron would actually get married at one point, but with the difference in age now, with her being older than him and having new goals, he started to understand. "I'm going to miss you, Saff."

"I'm going to miss you too, Jon." She reached in to grab him and they hugged. "If things were different, I think we could have made a good team."

That made him smile. "Me too," he answered.

They pulled apart and she gave him a quick kiss on the cheek, and then another hug. "You have a good one!" she wished him, before disappearing around the corner.

Jon walked into Boone's quarters. "You're the first one here, and we're waiting for the others," the Grand Admiral said. "We have our first mission with these Spearheads."

"What kind of mission, might I ask?"

"A simple jailbreak."

Two weeks later, the giant life-ship Ephesus began its journey into the stars carrying the Children of the Light. Several others had joined with the group in the intervening time, and there were also the Union officers and their families heading with them into a new world. Everyone knew that the journey would be long, but nobody knew just how long it would take.

That, however, is another story.

CHAPTER NINE

Past and Present

Thermonte Electrik did spend a lot of time thinking about his past these days. Things seemed to flash before his eyes, or his thoughts, one might say. He remembered the last time he had seen his first good friend, Derik Poe. It was just before he had him killed.

There had been a knock at the door, and in came his friend. He had just eaten dinner as he always did with Thermonte's family. He was living at the house, because Thermonte had promised him a more prominent position within the new syndicate.

"I think I found something for you, my friend," Thermonte told him. *"Leon is heading back to the Ofidian station, as you know, and he said he could use someone with your skills to take care of the entertainment on the station."*

Confused, Derik asked, "So what does that mean? Entertainment Director, something like that?"

Thermonte just smiled. "Exactly like that. I want someone I can trust, especially with the money part of it."

Derik thought about it for a moment. "It sounds good by me," he said. "First time off-world for me. It's exciting."

"I thought you would like it."

"When do we leave?"

"Leon is heading back there tonight, so you will need to get packed. You're going with him," Thermonte told him, and stood up and walked around his desk to stand in front of his childhood friend. "Gonna miss ya around here, though."

Derik just grinned gratefully. He held out his hand for a handshake, but Thermonte would have none of that. Instead, he pulled his friend close and gave him a hug, patting him on his back. Derik hugged him back. Nothing else was said, just a couple of nods, and Derik walked out to pack up for his trip.

Soon after Derik left, Leon walked in. "He's going?"

Thermonte nodded. "Yeah, you take care of him, okay?"

That was the last time he had seen Derik. He had also taken care of the man Derik had betrayed him to, Khanel Corlesh. He remembered how Khanel had looked when he had walked through the door where he was held. He remembered seeing his face covered with blood, dried blood. He was sitting in his chair, tied to it like an animal. Four of Thermonte's men sat around him laughing and smoking cigars, two of them playing a card game. It was evening and it was dark outside the building when his limo had driven up, and his men had straightened up as he had walked in, followed by his bodyguard.

Thermonte sat down across from his old boss, Khanel Corlesh, the last of the Corlesh Clan. "Do you know why you are still alive?"

Khanel looked around. He had been in this lifestyle long enough to know what would happen next. He kept his mouth shut.

"I personally killed your father," Thermonte told him. "I just wanted you to know that. Now what I want to know is, did you turn him?"

Khanel chuckled, then laughed as much as he could. "I treated him well. He kept me informed."

Thermonte stood up, and Khanel expected to die quickly, from a blast to the head. That was not the case. "Wrap it up," he told his men, and the four men each took a container of lithium fuel and doused the building. A circle around Khanel was left untouched. Then the four men followed their boss out the window, but the bodyguard moved in close to Khanel and stabbed him in the gut.

"Just in case," he whispered in his ear and left, throwing a lit

cigar on the fuel.

Thermonte Electrik and his men were well away from the building before the fire consumed it and the fire engineers showed up. Khanel's body was found more or less cooked, still tied to the chair.

He had to smile at that one. It was that event that made him a godfather, the Godfather. With that he had gotten respect. Another memory came to him, one where he tried to earn respect in another way. He had once tried to help one of the Corlesh clients, back on the world of Serenity.

He thought about it while waiting for the servants to come.

They called it The Underground, and it was located in the very heart of the city. The Underground contained many of the illegal activities that certain people looked for. Although those who visited checked their political differences at the door, it didn't keep them from getting into trouble here.

Thermonte had been sent there to see one man in particular. He was to collect some money from him that didn't quite make it to the Corlesh Clan. The man's name was Zac Fin. He ran an underground gambling facility during the overnight hours in Damascus, the capital city of Serenity.

Thermonte only took three of his men with him to the gambling facility, Leon Gar, Scotch Kammel, and Hester Boyd. Hester, the chief pilot of their ship, drove the air-car.

It was nearly dark when they set off. When they reached the facility, it had not quite opened yet. Soon Thermonte was sitting across from Zac in his office, and the gambling establishment was preparing to open.

Zac knew why Thermonte was there. The collected cut for the Corlesh Clan had been short by several thousand credits.

"So what is the problem?" Thermonte asked. Leon stood behind him and Scotch stood just outside the door, making sure they were not disturbed. "Mr. Corlesh wasn't too happy with last month's payment."

"Like I told the carrier, we had a slow month," Zac replied, a little worried about this visit. "Last month was a slow month for visitors."

"You know, it is regardless of your intake. Mr. Corlesh's cut is one hundred thousand credits per month. It's not a percentage thing," Thermonte explained. "You only sent him half that much."

"I needed the extra to keep this place running."

Thermonte sighed. "This month you owe him two hundred thousand."

"I can't pull that off. We have to pay off the Locals, so they don't raid the place, and that takes quite a bit," the man said. "I can still swing the one hundred thousand, though."

"I am afraid that won't work."

Thermonte once again considered his plan. Perhaps he could start something here that could help him in the future. "Perhaps we could come to some understanding, otherwise, you could be replaced."

Zac Fin seemed to make a strange noise at that prospect. He knew what replacement meant. "What is your proposal?"

"You put in your one hundred thousand and I will cover the rest. Now, if I do you this favor, I may want a favor in the future." Thermonte sat back and watched Zac as he thought about the proposal. Surely he would take it.

"What sort of favor?"

"In time," Thermonte told him. "In time. Don't worry, it will be something that will complement your talents."

Thermonte looked up at Leon, who just nodded. Leon knew all about his plans, about revenge, and he was all for it. He would rather have his boss in charge instead of that Corlesh boss. He was all behind Thermonte.

After another moment of thought, Zac Fin agreed to the deal. Leon turned and left, heading to the air-car, where Thermonte had left his case. A few minutes later, Leon was back and handing *him the case. Thermonte handed the case over to Zac.*

"Run this cash through your system and make it look as if it came from this world, and not from the mint. Do you have two hundred thousand already available?"

Zac replied, "It will take time to get it all together."

"How long?"

"Two hours."

Thermonte stood up. "Make it fast. And remember, this deal is between us only. Tell no one about this. Otherwise, Leon here might have to make a private visit."

"Don't worry," Zac replied. "I know that if Mr. Corlesh finds out, I'm a dead man, anyway."

As Thermonte and Leon left the room, Scotch asked a question. "So what's the deal?"

It was Leon who answered him back. "We're giving him a couple of hours to get the cash together." Then following Thermonte, he turned and said, "Come on, apparently the drinks are on the house."

Scotch followed. "Sounds good to me."

Two hours later, Thermonte Electrik walked back into Zac Fin's office ready for the payment of two hundred thousand to transport to San Corlesh. Scotch was in the room with them at this point.

Zac handed over the satchel containing the cash. Thermonte took it and looked inside. Then he handed it back to Scotch. "We will count it before we leave, Mr. Fin," he said as he stood up from the seat, reaching out to shake the man's hand. "Very nice to do business with you."

Once they were on board their ship, Thermonte called Leon into his compartment. "Well, what happened?"

"They might know, but it was never mentioned if they knew about your deal with Fin or not," explained Thermonte's friend and bodyguard. "Scotch went out to the car with Boyd for about an hour. Hints perhaps, but nothing definite."

"Keep it up. I want surveillance on them at all times. I just don't trust them as I should. Something is going on."

"I got people all around, boss. The network is building up pretty fast."

Thermonte was thinking all the time about this now. "Would we be able to act now if we need to?"

"Not quite, sir," Leon replied. "The network is becoming big, but we still don't have enough to act against the Clan."

Thermonte just nodded. "Okay then. Just keep me informed on what is going on. You are the most loyal friend I have," he told Leon. "Your loyalty will be well rewarded."

Servants were at the moment helping him dress in his imperial clothing, and now he was taking time to think about his humble start to becoming who he was today. He remembered meeting Doctor Phaleg for the first time like it was yesterday. It was at the Ikon shipyards so many years ago.

The shipyards were located on the far side of the three moons of Gin Kojoda, along the border of the Federation and the Republic. The world of Gin Kojodo was alone in the system but for the three moons that circled the planet one right after the other. An asteroid belt surrounded the planet and its moons, blocking some of the light from the system's sun. Daytime on Gin Kojoda was not particularly bright.

The primary base for the shipyards was located on the planet, surrounded by a large electrical fence. Within that fence were the only living people on the planet.

Thermonte brought Leon with him for a bit of muscle. They had taken a smaller long-distance shuttlecraft, since it was to be a quick trip. He found Joe Sharp in his office, and it seemed he was talking to another man.

The other man was a very tall, slender man, dressed in a very fine suit. His hair was black and slicked back. It was short and seemed to not have anything out of place. He turned around when Joe looked up, and saw them coming toward them. He had a big grin on his face, and his teeth looked as if they sparkled.

It Joe who spoke first. "You must be Thermonte Electrik,"

he said. *"Mister Corlesh called ahead and told me to expect you."*

"That's me," Thermonte said. *He walked toward the two men standing near a large waist-high table. He noticed that there were plans of a large ship on the table, almost as large as a battleship.*

The tall man looked over to him and offered his hand. "My name is Doctor Phaleg," he said, and he wrapped his long fingers around Thermonte's hand. It made Thermonte almost feel weird.

"I'm supposed to design and have a ship built for him," Joe told the doctor. "A gift from his employer."

"Ahh," smiled Phaleg. "I know Mister Corlesh well. We are discussing a viable business proposition."

Thermonte grunted lightly. "I have heard nothing about it."

"No one has as yet. It's only between us." Then to Joe he said, "Perhaps I should go and let you two get to work. My ship can wait, let's get this man's ship built."

That was his first meeting with the good Doctor Phaleg. It was at his second meeting when deals were struck, and when he had been recruited into the great plan to take control of the galaxy. He had come a long way since then, however. He had become someone important, someone with much influence. He smiled as he thought back.

He stood up and returned the handshake Phaleg had offered.

Thermonte was smiling. "I've not done so bad."

"You've taken over the Corlesh Clan and restructured it to fit your own needs. Well done, my friend." Doctor Phaleg sat across from Thermonte at his desk.

"Man has to make a living."

After they were relaxed and drinks had been served, it was Phaleg that started the next conversation. "So it seems you might have some trouble with the House of Taran?"

"Yea, well, we're staying ahead of them for now."

"I can help," Phaleg quickly replied, "and they will not connect it to you. I guarantee it."

"I'm intrigued." Thermonte sat and thought for a moment. What would this cost him, he wondered. "So what do I have to do for you to repay you?"

Phaleg smiled. "You have to do nothing for me. I just want to start a working relationship with you. Nothing more. I like your style, Mr. Electrik."

"What would this relationship include?"

"No money involved," promised the man. "You need a favor for something like this House of Taran thing, and in return, I may ask you for a favor."

"What is your business?"

"I am planning an exploration trip, so far deep into unknown space it will take nearly two or three years in an FTL ship to get *there."*

Thermonte raised his brow. "Sounds interesting. What is an FTL ship?"

"Faster Than Light."

The godfather laughed. "There is no such thing."

Phaleg held up a single finger in hopes to quiet Thermonte's laugh. "Do you remember the first time we met?"

Thermonte remembered.

"I was there ordering the ship to be built for that trip, and now it is ready."

"You mean it goes faster than light?" Thermonte was still skeptical.

"No, no, of course not," Phaleg answered. "The ship has been built, but I have a scientist and engineers working on the engines themselves, on a world I call Dragmar."

"Where is this Dragmar?"

"A week outside of the known galaxy at lightspeed."

Phaleg had told him a lot, and Thermonte knew this. "So, what favors would I do for you?"

"Well, for now, through your business and connections, I could use someone to help recruit for this trip. And I would need people with no families or anything like that. I don't mind the criminal element, but they need to be the best at what they do."

After several minutes, Thermonte thought he might give this a try. *"Sounds like an okay deal. Do you have a recruit in mind?"*

"So I take it this is a yes, my friend?"

Thermonte extended his hand. Both shook on the deal. "It is a yes. So who do you have in mind first?"

"There is a rising star within the Federation Navy. A man named Gedor. He is a foolish man, but he is the best at what he does best." Phaleg just smiled. "Being a fool."

"And where is the best place to find this man?"

"I believe he is the threat the House of Taran warned you about. So he may come to you."

As they concluded their visit, and Doctor Phaleg was about to leave, Thermonte asked him a question. "About this exploratory trip you have planned, what is out there? What do you hope to find?"

Doctor Phaleg just smiled that smile. "Water, my friend, and I know it is out there. I just got to get there."

They had found it, and had been to the planet ten years ago, and Thermonte himself had been transported back to Bel Terra through what he called the Space Gate. The others were left behind on the far-away world. He was told that Doctor Phaleg had been killed just before the Space Gate had been destroyed from the other end. He only wished he could have brought Soshiana back with him. But soon, he felt, he would see her again.

Back on the base on Dust, the Union leaders held a meeting discussing what their first move involving the new Spearhead ships would be. Grand Admiral Boone was there, as well as Jon and Nicolea and others. General Long, Commander Astarte, and Commander Sal Ganat were also present. Sal Ganat had just been given command of his own ship.

"We should launch an attack against Bel Terra and destroy the head of the snake," someone was saying. Jon couldn't see, but it sounded like General Long.

Nicolea spoke up then. "I don't think Mister Electrik is the problem. He definitely was not in charge back on Khair Din."

"I agree," Jon piped in. "As much as I dislike the fat ol' criminal, and despise his actions, I think there is more to it than this."

"But it is where everyone thinks the power lies," Stanton said. "It could help with the ongoing uprising."

"True," Boone replied. He caught a glimpse of an empty chair in the back of the room, and an image of his brother came to mind. "It could also cause us to have to dig deeper to find the real core of this evil."

At that moment Soshiana, who had been standing at Nicolea's left, stepped slightly forward. Jon had not even known she was there. She was a stealthy little woman. "No one touch Thermonte Electrik," she said softly. I need to talk to him first, and maybe I could find out who is really running this empire."

"How can we know that we can trust her?" piped in a voice from yet another contributor. "She did work for him, you know."

"I trust her," Jon said surprisingly, and he noticed Nicolea looking his way, smiling.

"So do I," replied Boone. "Since she has been here, she has been an asset to us."

There was a long quiet moment, where men and women murmured among themselves. Commander Astarte spoke up then, with his thick accent. Jon thought it was much thicker than Nicolea's had ever been.

"That still leaves us on what our first move should be against the Pagonic Empire," he said. "I know we are all eager to finally be able to attack first for a change."

Everyone sounded their agreement. Then Solomon said, "I have an idea about that." He paused until the room became silent. "Since these ships have a sort of stealth technology, a surprise attack would be a perfect start."

Again, everyone murmured their agreement.

"We attack Black Star."

The room fell silent again, as the thought behind it seeped in. Commander Ganat spoke his first words since the meeting began. "How does attacking a prison help us fight a war against the Imperium?"

Boone smiled. "Good question, and glad you asked," he said as he activated the holo-map on the table behind him and walked around to the other side. The others followed to get a closer look at the plan.

There was a holo-representation of the Black Star prison at its center. "We all know that many of our finest are being held there, including General Brande. We would jump in close, quickly send out shuttlecrafts to every docking port, and move in from every angle. While we are releasing our men from their cells, another group will go in and take the control room at its center, and download any and all files from the computer. As we move out, we plant explosives throughout. Once we are all back on board the Spearheads, we detonate the explosives."

Another man asked, "You know that Black Star is the highest maximum security prison in the known galaxy?"

"Stealth tech," Long replied quickly. "Our arrival won't be detected, and we're working on a way to get in the docking bays, too. They won't know we are there until we are inside."

"And it is because of that very reason," Admiral Boone pointed at the man, "that they will not be expecting this attack. Just think of the intel we can get from the computer of the Black Star. You know it holds secrets."

After a brief discussion back and forth of the pros and cons, the mission to attack and free the prisoners was agreed upon. As everyone left the room, Solomon Boone looked over at Jon, who had stayed behind for just a moment. "I knew that you coming home was a good omen, Jon."

Jon slightly smiled, then asked, "Do you believe we will win this war, Admiral?"

"This is just the first battle we have been able to initiate," he said back. "I don't know how long this war will last, but with the Lord of Light on our side, we have to win. But it's not going to be easy."

Jon believed that they would. He left then and went his way.

Soshiana was on Nicolea's left side as they walked down the corridor. "When will we head for Bel Terra?" she asked him.

"A little anxious, are you?"

"I remember who I am, and this memory needs to be shared," she replied. "I have read all your books and scrolls in your bag, and I have talked at length with you about becoming a true believer of the Light, and I believe with what I tend to think of as my heart, that I am now a Child of Light. Now, whether or not I can get onto the Shores of Paradise, and the City of Light, I don't really know, because I am a bio-tek, an abomination, hated by the Light. But I will believe that I can make a difference on this physical world and I am giving all I have to the Lord of Light.

"It is all I know to do," she continued. "I just hope I can do what I have to do before these computers inside of me take over, if they will. I know my real side desires the Light, but will the computer in me stop my longing for the Light?"

If she hadn't been a bio-tek, Nicolea would have thought she had been crying tears down her face. But she was a bio-tek, and she was right. Nothing like this had ever happened, and only the Lord of Light knew what she truly was. He knew he believed in her. He also knew there was more to understand before he could give her a definite answer. He was just beginning his journey as well.

"You will be just fine," he assured her. In the end, he knew it would all be alright.

He reached over and did what he thought would comfort her. He drew her in and hugged her. He also knew he was being summoned to Illosha and he would probably bring her along. Perhaps they would find out something there.

"We will leave as soon as this mission is over," he promised. "I am sure, He believes in you."

CHAPTER TEN
Salvation

Several months later, the Union sent out a small fleet of Spearheads for their planned rescue mission on the Black Star prison. In the time before the Imperium, Black Star was a prison which contained only the deadliest of criminals, assassins, and terrorists. Now it housed those who stood against the Imperium. The rescue mission was to rescue the Union supporters like General Brande, who was once Jon's superior during the Republic.

From a distance, Black Star looked much like a black sphere constructed like a spider's web. One black orb with six outstretched fingers connected to another orb, and so on. Each orb contained a group of prison cells. They all connected to the larger orb in the very center. This central orb contained everything else. According to Union intelligence, a vast quantity of Bathshe still survived here, kept until needed for later. The Union had never really believed the Bathshe had ever left or died out.

Seven Spearhead battleships jumped back into real space just next to the Black Star prison. As soon as possible, two shuttlecrafts from each ship departed and headed for one of the fourteen docking bays within the cluster of the prison. On board one of the shuttles from the Spearhead ship Dakota were Jon, Nicolea, Soshiana, and some Union soldiers.

Dressed in Union armor and ready for a fight, Jon was the first to leave the shuttle once it had landed. The battle began almost immediately. Soshiana was out of the shuttle right after Jon, using all of her skills as a bio-tek fighting against the Bathshe and human Imperium troops. Following the Union soldiers, Nicolea stepped out, now wearing the robes Lenok once wore. After this mission, he would have to leave for Illosha.

The troops streaming into the docking bay were quickly taken care of. Jon's team moved on and began to slowly make their way deeper into the prison. Getting off of another shuttle was Ben Gettel, leading another assault in another docking bay. With him was a woman they called Tekk. She was a hacker and a genius with software and hardware. Tekk was more of a nickname really; she never gave up her real name.

Ben led his team slowly to the center of the prison. There, Tekk would be able to do her best work. Deeper within the prison, those in control sent out a distress call once the fight inside began. All Pagonic troops at the prison, both human and Bathshe, were being sent to try and stop the Union soldiers from advancing. With every kill of a Bathshe, a strange scream seemed to resonate from the dying giants.

Captain Finch from the Dakota called Jon and Ben to keep in touch with what was going on. Just outside the docking bay in the corridor, Jon and his team seemed to get bogged down.

Soshiana looked around them. She noticed the ventilation system vent above them. It was small, but with her physique she could easily crawl through. "I have an idea," she told the others, and commenced to move into the vent and disappear.

Even though Nicolea had become known for being a spiritual leader, he was still willing to fight. He moved up to take Soshiana's place, firing the automatic Stinger rifle. It was the same kind he had once used protecting the Federation. "How much further in do you think we need to go for the General and Cas Barnes?"

"According to the intel, we have two more of these corridors to get through," Jon answered. "They are in cell block 12."

They saw a flash ahead, then heard several small explosions. Jon looked at his friend. "She made it." Then, waving his arm forward, he motioned for his team to advance up to the first group of cells. Moving slowly through, the team checked every cell; all of them were empty.

Soshiana was standing there waiting for them at the entrance to the next corridor. "Take your time, why don't you," she said with a grin.

"Is this the right one?" Jon asked her, and she nodded. Each group of cells had five exits leading to more groups of cells. "I need two men to stay here and let us know if and when more troops arrive."

A few moments later they were in another firefight. Soshiana looked around but found no vent near them. They would have to find another way through. She laid the palm of her hand on the floor and sent out a pulse, mapping out a portion of the structure around them. After a few moments of studying the map in her mind, she said, "I found a way around."

Jon ordered his team to keep fighting their way through, then he and Nicolea followed Soshiana around the long way.

The other teams were making similar progress all over the prison. The Black Star housed about two thousand staff, including soldiers and Bathshe and techs, and about three thousand prisoners when it was at peak capacity. As more and more of the Pagonic side fell, the Union found it increasingly easy to advance. With all the fighting from the other teams, Ben and his team found it easier to make it to the prison's core, where the computer system was housed.

Once they reached the core, Tekk got to work on the nearest terminal, which lit up above the table. The soldiers moved into position to defend her and her work.

Captain Finch, as well as the six captains of the other Spearhead battleships, monitored their teams and kept them updated on the situation outside of the prison. It was only about forty-five minutes into the mission, when a Pagonic Imperium ship jumped in. It was the largest battleship any of them had ever seen. It was a Pagonic Dreadnought Destroyer, the Brimstone, the first one they had ever come across. It looked like an 'M' with long arms on the sides stretching out towards the front. Four sets of wings, like those of a bat, curved back toward the engines. The central section had twenty-five levels, and a small protrusion at the front. Harbinger fighters came swarming out from the docking bays located in the outer arms.

The Dakota and the other battleships released the newly redesigned Ikon fighters, which came with the battleships from the Utopian shipyards. The fighters clashing together and bursts of laser light thickened the view between the enemies.

"You guys need to hurry," Captain Finch said over the comms to Jon and the others. "You're not going to believe the size of this ship. It's much bigger than all seven of our battleships together. If another one shows up, we're done for."

Jon replied back, "We've almost gotten our prisoners out, I'm not sure about Ben and the others. What about the other teams throughout?"

"Some of the teams are already back on their ships," Finch replied. "Hurry, we have a fight, and I don't think we can make it too long."

As Tekk was copying the information off of the computer system, she noticed a strange file. It was a location file for a galactic map labeled Mammon. She called Ben over to look at it.

"Never heard of it," Ben answered her. "We'll look at it later, we got to get back to the Dakota."

She agreed, and within minutes everything they needed had been copied. They headed back to their shuttle in one of the outer bays, following the same route back they had taken to get there.

Jon, Nicolea, and Soshiana had taken the long way, and had found their two prisoners. General Brande looked a little haggard and underweight, but he was extremely glad when he saw Jon. It had been a long time since he had seen his friend.

Brande was so glad to see Jon, he actually hugged him. "My boy," he started, "I thought you were dead and gone a long time ago. Praise the Lord of Light you still live."

"Don't forget about me," came a voice on the opposite side. It was Cas Barnes.

Brande introduced Cas to them, and then they released the others that were housed within the cell block. Then they made their way back, met up with their team, and headed back to the shuttle. The reunion was cut short on the docking bay as the battle outside continued.

Captain Finch contacted the other Spearheads, finding out there were two more shuttles that had not yet made it back. It was the crews of these shuttles that were planting Titan explosives throughout the prison facility. Four of the seven Spearheads were now engaging in battle, taking out the Harbinger fighters and trying to attack the Brimstone. The Brimstone only took minor damage, but the Harbinger fighters were being wiped out quickly.

The last two shuttles came out from Black Star just as the Titan explosives tore apart the prison. Multiple explosions shot out. The Brimstone began moving back, calling most of their fighters back as well. Some of their fighters had gotten too close and were caught in the explosions.

Finch and the other captains used this to move their ships back, and once all the shuttles were on board, they all turned and shot into hyperspace, heading for the bulk of their fleet just outside the known galactic civilization.

Sitting around a table in the canteen on the Dakota, Cas Barnes and General Brande were eating their first decent meal since being imprisoned. Sitting with them were Jon, Soshiana, and Captain Finch. According to Soshiana, Nicolea was in his quarters in meditation praying to the Lord of Light.

"These new battleships are fantastic," Brande said, looking around at the others in the room. Most of them were the prisoners they had rescued from the same cell block. "How many of these ship do you have?"

"About thirty," Finch replied. Then he told them the entire find at the Utopian shipyards. "They are not all active quite yet, we need to continue to train the crews and bring them over from the Dust base. Once that's done, we'll be able to attack the Imperium in multiple places at once."

"So we'll be able to attack instead of just doing patrols and small raids," Brande mused. "A new era in our fighting against the darkness."

Several minutes later, Nicolea walked in and came right up to their table. "Jon, I need to talk to you," he said, as Jon stood up and followed him to an empty table.

They sat down. "What's on your mind?" Jon asked him.

"As soon as we get back to the Dust base, Soshiana and I will be leaving for Illosha on the Chimera."

Jon said, "You mean Thermonte Electrik's yacht?"

"I got a good feeling it will get us past security on Bel Terra."

"It might get you more than that." Jon was smiling at him. Then he said, "I was hoping you would stick around for a while."

"Well, I've got some time now," Nicolea told him. "What's on your mind?"

Jon grew serious, and after a short pause he said, "I want to get saved. I want to secure my soul to the Light. Tell me how to do that."

Nicolea smiled. Finally his friend had accepted and had asked of him the one thing he wanted to hear. "First you must believe with all your heart and soul that the Son of Light died for our sin and rose again to conquer all sin."

"After the things I have been through and seen with my own eyes, the things Iosa can do through prayer, I do believe." Jon told him. "But it's more than that."

"Like what?"

"Not quite sure," Jon replied.

Nicolea smiled. "You will learn as you go. Maybe we should get Mister Barnes. He is the Union spiritual leader. It would be good for him to get back in the swing of things, and with a new convert also."

"But you're a Prophet Warrior," Jon said.

"I have not been commissioned as of yet," Nicolea replied. "That is one reason I need to go back to Illosha."

After a few moments of silence and thinking, Jon finally agreed to go with him to talk to Cas Barnes. He would have to make his decision public and start his new life with the first act of obedience. His life didn't belong to himself, but to the Lord of Light.

Many had gathered in the room they had been using as the sanctuary for their Church of Light on the Dust base. Nicolea stood facing the altar where Jon was about to be immersed in water, symbolizing the burial and resurrection of Iosa. Behind him stood most of Jon's friends and some fellow believers Jon had not yet met. Standing with Jon was their shepherd for the Union, Cas Barnes.

Cas Barnes and Jon stood in a giant tub of water, about waist high. As Cas began speaking, an officer from the main control room entered the sanctuary. He looked around and found Admiral Boone standing with the others.

He walked up and tapped him on the shoulder.

"What is it?" Solomon whispered.

"We have Pagonic battleships and dreadnoughts heading for Dust. They have several destroyers with them."

Solomon leaned close to his man, as his eye caught the eye of General Brande. "Begin evacuation process and scatter the new fleet. We'll have to fight until everyone is away."

The officer nodded, and ran out to do his job. As the ceremony ended, and Jon was lifted up out of the water after being dunked, the base took several hits from the enemy above. The alarms sounded and the evacuation plan was underway.

Jon jumped out of the tub and ran out with the rest to help with the evacuation with a new vigor and a new hope for the future. As the base buzzed like a disturbed ant hill, above the planet the Spearhead battleships engaged the attacking Pagonic ships. The giant destroyers who came in behind the dreadnoughts continued to pound the base below.

Back inside the base, Nicolea grabbed Jon by the arm as he ran by. "We're heading out in the yacht, back to Bel Terra and Illosha."

Jon nodded and gave him a quick hug. "Don't be a stranger, Nic," he said, accepting that his friend had to leave.

"Don't worry," replied Nicolea, "we'll see one another again."

They both nodded, and then Jon was running again.

Nicolea turned back toward Soshiana after watching his friend disappear into the crowd. "Let's go," he told her, and they made their way to the Chimera.

As they left the docking bay, they could see the surrounding forest burning. They stayed close to the surface of the planet until they were away from the battle, and then they headed up into the stars and made their jump to Bel Terra.

CHAPTER ELEVEN
Into The Fire

As the Chimera made its way to Bel Terra, Soshiana and Nicolea both sat in the galley as she continued to tell him of her thoughts on entering Illosha. Both knew what had to be done.

After swallowing a bite of sandwich, Nicolea replied. "I don't know. You are a special case. There has never been a bio-tek that has survived as long as you have. Not one has been saved from the darkness as you have. You have to confront your fears and we need to make sure you are truly accepted by the Way of the Light. So in this world, this reality, you must have this trial."

"What if I don't pass? What will happen to me?"

"If you are truly saved, then you have nothing to worry about. Don't fear the outcome of this trial, my friend. For if you know in your heart that you are saved, it will all be a breeze."

Soshiana bit into the sandwich Nicolea had made for her. It was only a half sandwich, for she had only recently begun eating. While eating was still possible for a bio-tek, it was not necessary. Soshiana had been trying to embrace her more human aspects, one of which was eating food. She chewed then swallowed, taking a quick sip of water to chase the bread down her throat. "Not bad," she said. "Much milder than the other stuff I've tried."

"No matter what the outcome of your trial, you will still need to slowly get back into the swing of things like eating."

She nodded in agreement. Her stomach had not been used for eating in a long time. It did worry her what it was being used for now, and what lay within. "Do you think this could all be fixed, physically I mean, on that island of Illosha you told me about?"

"If that is what is meant to happen, I say so," Nicolea replied with a smile. "If there is one place that can reverse your situation, Illosha is that place."

An alarm sounded from the speakers overhead, and Soshiana knew what that meant. Bel Terra was close and it was time to jump back into normal space. They had left Dust nearly a week ago, and in her eyes, things were almost at an end. Both of them headed for the bridge.

The Chimera jumped into normal space above the world of Bel Terra. There were many other ships, both larger pleasure ships and private yachts, waiting above the planet for their turn to land. Soshiana looked at the galactic date on the screen, and it confirmed what she thought.

There was a ceremony in the capital city on Bel Terra to honor the emperor and the Imperium tomorrow. These ships were those who were coming to attend the ceremony and pay their tribute to Thermonte Electrik, Emperor of the Galaxy.

A moment later two Pagonic fighters came up beside the Chimera, and one of the pilots spoke to them. "Chimera, we need confirmation of passengers on board before you can be permitted to land by the Palace Authority. Will you comply?"

"Just two passengers," replied Soshiana into the mic.

"Names and ranks, if any," one of the pilots requested.

"I am Soshiana, and my companion is Nicolea Dan," she looked back at him, looking him over, then smiled. "He is a scribe."

There was a moment of silence. Then, with a more

relaxed voice, the fighter pilot said, "Soshiana, His Majesty, the Emperor Electrik, has been waiting long for your homecoming. You and your companion are welcome to land in the private landing platform near the palace. Please follow us as we will escort you in."

"We'll follow you then," Soshiana answered them as one of them took the lead in front.

The pilot spoke again in the same manner. "I was just informed that Andrelus Pan will meet you on the platform and escort you to the emperor once you have set down. He is most anxious to greet you."

Soshiana looked back at Nicolea with a worried look on her face. Facing her fears was coming sooner than she thought. "Thank you," she replied, as Nicolea gave her a comforting smile and nod.

The Chimera jumped to the front of the line, and followed the lead fighter down onto the planet and near the palace. Once they set down on the platform and shut down the ship, Soshiana led the way and Nicolea followed. He had the hood of the cloak he now wore up over his head, and carried his satchel strapped across his back. Andrelus Pan came out from the shadow of the entrance and met them halfway, followed by six armed soldiers.

"Welcome home, Soshiana," Andrelus said to her, looking her over. He remembered her from somewhere, but wasn't quite sure where. "I must inform you that weapons are not permitted here in the palace. If you have any on your person, we need to confiscate them until you leave. It's for the safety of the Emperor, you see."

Soshiana retrieved her pistol she wore down by her side and the knife belt she had around her waist. "Of course," she said, and handed those weapons to one of the soldiers with Andrelus.

"I understand you are a bio-tek …."

Soshiana interrupted him. "I am, and everything else is a part of me, so in order for you to confiscate anything else, you will have to kill me first. I don't think the emperor will like that."

Andrelus really did not care, but he said, "Of course." Then he turned his attention to Nicolea. "Search him."

Nicolea held his arms outstretched to allow the search. "What's in the bag?" the soldiers searching him asked him.

"Papers and book," Nicolea replied. "I am a scribe, after all."

They took a peek in the satchel and confirmed that there were no weapons. Andrelus smiled and led them into the palace. The six soldiers walked on either side of Soshiana and Nicolea, as Andrelus led them through a series of wide, long corridors, heading toward the entrance of the palace.

They came to a giant foyer with large doors on either side, waiting benches sitting between the doors. At the fourth door, furthest from the entrance, they stopped.

Andrelus turned. "Emperor Electrik is in here waiting to see you, Soshiana," he said. "You, sir, may wait out here for her." He motioned toward the benches in a friendly manner.

Nicolea knew who this man was. Thermonte had told him and Jon about him all those years ago in his home on Chotis. Nicolea just smiled and nodded in agreement at Andrelus, and sat down on the bench next to the door.

"The soldiers will stand watch while you talk with our esteemed emperor," Andrelus told Soshiana. "They will be just outside the door if you need them."

"Thank you," she answered.

Andrelus just smiled as he watched her enter the door and it closed behind her. Then to Nicolea he said,

"I have other duties which I need to take care of before the ceremony tomorrow, if you will excuse me."

Nicolea smiled and replied with a nod.

"If you need me for anything, just ask one of the soldiers. They know how to get ahold of me."

"Thank you," was Nicolea's reply, and Andrelus left, the sound of his footsteps echoing as he moved away.

Thermonte Electrik was dressed in his finest clothing. He had been very excited when he found out the Chimera was over the planet. He wanted to be seen just right for his dear companion's return. He had a small feast brought into his private dining hall, where he waited for her. The closer she came, the more nervous tension grabbed him. He began eating the food and drinking the wine. He ate fast due to the tension, but he wanted to show her the wealth he had accumulated, and just what being emperor really meant. Now that he could have anything he wanted, and she had returned, she would be a part of that.

She was that loyal, and she would be rewarded. The door opened.

Soshiana stood just inside the room, looking at her former employer, as the door closed behind her. Not much seemed to have changed. He still liked to eat and drink, but without her regulating it for him, well, it had gotten out of hand.

He looked up and smiled. "Soshiana, my dear friend and companion. My most loyal of servants, come on in, and talk to me. I have missed you," he said.

"I can tell," she answered. "You're fat. Very fat."

Thermonte smiled. Her words were music to his ears. He took a drink of wine, gulping it down, and poured himself another glass. "I have missed you."

"Then why did you leave me behind?" she asked him bluntly. She had never been one to mince words when she was around him. It was something he liked about her.

"It was a rash decision on my part. But be glad that I did, because you would not have survived the journey through the gate."

"Who told you that?"

"The builders of the gate." Thermonte replied. "I also knew that since you are a bio-tek, you could survive the journey back with no trouble. It was the waiting that was the hard part, the part I had to endure. You know you are the only one that I can trust." Then in a loud whisper, he leaned in and said, "I've started to not get much respect from anyone around here, and I don't think they like me. That's why I am having this tribute ceremony tomorrow. Perhaps it will show them just how important I really am."

"Sorry it took me so long," she said.

A concerned look came across his face. "What exactly did take you so long? I already had the return coordinates set."

"It was all a setup. They took out the FTL engines and all we were left with were the light drive engines."

"We?"

"Jon Vega and Nicolea Dan."

"I remember them."

"He's outside waiting for me."

"You mean Nicolea Dan. He was not always a scribe." He had heard Andrelus call to find out who all was on the Chimera. "Well, I suppose he will have his use." Then as an afterthought he said, "Perhaps he could write down the story of my life, write my biography."

She watched him eat more food and drink more wine. Nicolea was not that kind of scribe. Then she asked, "Have you ever thought about turning your life around and being a Child of Light?"

Thermonte nearly choked on the food in his mouth. "You're starting to sound like my mother, the dear sweet lady she was. Why do you ask that?"

"Something I have been learning about on my journey home."

Thermonte then remembered. "That Lenok fellow told you about Him."

"He was killed back on Khair Din, but I read his scrolls and learned a lot. Also, Nicolea helped me. Now I am a Child of the Light."

Thermonte nearly choked again. "You're being funny. Being a Child of Light is forbidden in the Imperium. Come to me, Soshiana, and let us be like we used to. I need a trusted ally in this place. I need you. Besides, you're just a bio-tek."

Soshiana moved in closer so that she was standing next to him. "You need to take this seriously. I bet you don't even know who I am?"

"You are my friend, my helper, and my bio-tek," answered Thermonte.

Soshiana looked at him. "Can you be that stupid as to not know the meaning of the name Soshiana?"

Thermonte looked at her strangely. "It is just a name, yes?"

"It is from an ancient tongue. Soshi means 'daughter of.' Surely you can guess the next part."

"Ana," he smiled, saying it, proving his mind was sharp. Then he thought about it more. Daughter of Ana. Another spelling would be Anna. He looked at her again in a slightly different light, wondering. *Could it have all been a setup? Was he that ignorant?*

Soshiana confirmed what he was thinking. "I am your daughter, father," she said slowly. "I no longer rely on this bio-tek side of me. Doctor Phaleg found me and tricked me, and I became this thing to be given to you. The connection I felt toward you, the loyalty, was true, because you were my father. It's one of the reasons I have lasted so long as a bio-tek."

"Then, daughter, let us take what is ours," he replied. "I want you next to my side as we, together, rule this Imperium. This is our kingdom, and it's our time to rule. I will be able to provide and give you anything you will ever want."

"I am sorry, sir," she simply said. "I will give you one last chance to accept the Way of the Light, as I have. Let the Light save your soul."

"What has the Light ever done for me?" Thermonte cried. "Nothing. I got here all on my own, and I will grow even stronger all on my own. My soul is satisfied."

From a hidden compartment in the back of Soshiana's neck, she reached up and withdrew a small slender knife with a rigid blade. She leaned in close to him. "You are too fat, father, and there is nothing more I can do for you."

With that she plunged the blade into Thermonte's gut. He had gotten so fat that the entire knife was drawn deep into his gut with his last few breaths. Without even a tear coming from her eyes, she left the room, back out into the giant foyer. The soldiers looked at her as she came out, and Nicolea stood watching.

"He will need a few moments alone," she told them. "My companion and I need an escort to find our way to the front gate."

The soldier left in charge pointed to two of his men to continue to guard the door until his return. Then he and the others led her and Nicolea to the front gate of the palace, where they grabbed an air-cab and made their way to the local hover-train station. Perhaps she would shed a tear for her father later.

Thermonte Electrik stopped chewing. His eyes stopped blinking as he watched his daughter walk out of the room. Betrayed by his own flesh and blood, she had been with him this entire time. He had felt the slice the knife made as it cut through his flesh. He could feel the movement of the knife as it moved deeper into his body with each breath he tried to take. He could feel each breath getting shallower. He could even feel the blood that came out of the wound, little as it was, to stain his royal clothing.

He didn't care that the food fell out of his mouth and onto the floor. His eyesight was getting worse and worse, and his movement stiffened. He knew however, that he was falling forward onto the table of his own feast that was laid out before him. He was scared. Before his head hit the table everything went dark and the pain was gone.

Then his eyes opened and pain upon pain consumed him. All around him, he felt fire ravage his body, but his body was not consumed. His mind was filling with the agony and the pain. He wanted to cry, but tears boiled away before they made it out of his tear ducts. The torture was continuous and he knew it would never end.

He looked up, as from a pit, and there he saw his mother, looking down on him from the top of the pit. "Help me, Mother!" he cried. "Please, Mother, help me!

It's me, Thermonte, your little boy!" He reached out to her, but all she did was stare back at him with a solemn look on her face.

She turned then, and he never saw her again.

CHAPTER TWELVE

A New Life

Nicolea and Soshiana moved to the local hover-train station and took the overnight train to the city of Brickersville, the northern coastal city near the North Sea.

"Before the expansion of man into space, Brickersville was once known as Bordertown," Nicolea told her, but she was in her own thoughts.

She began to wonder about the past, or the 'what if' about the past. About Mister Electrik, her father, a man she never knew fully. She once worked for him under the influence of the bio-tek mind, but now she was free of all that. It was because of Mister Electrik that she was where she was. Or was it?

She remembered a time before being placed in the hands of the bio-tek way. She tried hard to remember a name. *Just what was it?*

The Eastern Starlight Resort. That was the name of it. It was the hottest vacation and holiday spot in the Republic, located on the world of Achillon. The finest luxury hotel known was surrounded by the peaceful, tropical Gravelgan Forest. Visitors would fly into the private space bays just behind the resort. Soshiana was co-owner and she had lived there and had run the place. At least, she did back when she was Alexeena Electrik.

She remembered asking her mom if she could change her surname, but her mother had told her, "If you do good with that name, maybe it will balance out what your father does. You were born with that name, and the Lord of Light blessed you with it. Do something good with it."

Perhaps she should have visited her father, maybe that would have changed things, made him a better person.

Alexeena was her name. No, it *is* her name. From here on out, she thought, she would no longer be known as Soshiana, but as Alexeena.

Nicolea watched her in her thoughts, and held his tongue. She wasn't interested in the history of Bel Terra, especially after what she had just been through. Until she was ready to talk about it, he wouldn't push her. He was here when she needed him. He reached into his satchel and pulled out the scroll he had been reading. It would pass his time and give him a deeper knowledge of the past.

Lenok then found Stark, Manis, and Kanis, and they led the people of the Light out from the city of Ashkeloth and through the mountains of Erish. They followed the small river to one of the lakes of Tarkoon, and then made their way to the eastern shore of one of the other lakes, which was between the twin lakes. There they made camp, abiding there for a year.

It was within that year that Stark, Manis, and Kanis learned the ways of the Ghel people and became integrated with them. They read and understood the Law of the Light and they stood in understanding of the Grace they had received from the Light. They followed in obedience to the immersion in water as the acknowledgment that the Light shone within. Stark, Manis, and Kanis became part of the Ghel.

After the year was spent, they gathered their belongings back into their caravan and traveled into the north entrance of the forest of Hilborne.

Now the king who sat on the throne in Hilborne Castle heard of the passing of the Ghel people and sent emissaries out to greet them in the forest.

Lenok spoke to the emissary, who said, "The king of Hilborne requests that you give tribute to cross our land and into the land that you seek, before thou cross any further."

"I must have till the morrow to pray to the Light about the tribute," was Lenok's answer.

"Do not leave the path of this forest," replied the emissary. "For our soldiers await at the path's end, in case thou refuse to pay tribute."

That evening, the White Seraph appeared again to the Prophet Warrior and said, "When the dark comes and the mist clouds the vision of the soldiers, take the people west across Westborne to the shore of the Southern Sea. There, they will be saved."

The sun lowered into the sky and a thick mist descended, and it was then that Lenok led the Ghel people westward through the forest, led by faith and surrounded by the mist. It was daylight when they reached the shore of the sea there. They rested then.

When the emissary saw that the Ghel people were gone, he reported back to the king of Hilborne. The king's heart hardened, and he sent his soldiers out to find and destroy the Ghel people.

When Lenok and the rest of the Ghel people heard that the Hilborne soldiers were on their way, the people began to fret and worry. Lenok then picked a man after the Lord of Light's own heart, whose name was Jael. He was to lead the people to the island that lay ahead.

"That island is so far out and we can't walk on water," Jael replied, telling him of the people's troubles.

Lenok took his staff and placed the head of the staff on the water and prayed to the Lord of the Light. The sea then parted, leaving a dry path to the island with giant walls of water rising on either side. The Ghel people began to move then, across the dry land heading to the land that was promised to them by the Lord of Light, the God of all Creation.

As the last of the Ghel crossed the sea, the scout for the Hilborne soldiers saw, and went back and told the captain of the army, and when he had heard, he gathered the army and they headed hard for the Ghel and followed them across the dry path.

Now when the people had crossed the dry path of the sea, and the soldiers were halfway across, the giant walls of water crashed down onto the Hilborne soldiers and killed them all.

The Ghel people were saved and now they were in the land of their inheritance. The land they called the Isle of Tesh. It contained three larger bodies of water connected by grassy channels between each one. The first one they called Imaelan. The second one they called Jamaelan, and the third they named Kamaelan. These were named after the first cities from the ancient times given to them by the White Seraph.

The Ghel people lived in peace for a time, and Jael was their judge.

Nicolea and Alexeena climbed off of the train and made their way to a local restaurant for something to eat. Then they gathered provisions and rented an air-car and headed toward the northern beaches.

"I'm here to talk about what happened, when you're ready," he told her.

She smiled. Nicolea had been her mentor and friend ever since they had left Khair Din, and it was because of Nicolea that she had gotten saved into the Light. "Well," she started, "it's like ending one life and beginning another. I never knew my father, so I don't really know how to feel about him now that he is dead."

"No point in dwelling too deep on it. He made his choices in life, and it led him there. It may not have been anything you did or didn't do to save him. All you can do now is work on your own life. You are free of the bio-tek lifestyle, now it's time for you to make your own decisions and follow in the way of the Light."

They reached their destination in about an hour and a half, and then made their way to the sandy beaches of Northshire, where the waves were gently rolling in.

"Do you think I will be welcomed?" Alexeena asked him.

Nicolea thought for a moment. "I guess we'll have to wait on Rosha. I'm sure he will let us know."

"Rosha?"

"The boatman that will carry us from these shores to Illosha."

"I don't see anyone here," she said, looking up and down the shoreline. Even though Bel Terra had been becoming more populated since the Imperium had come into existence, these northern sands had yet to be really discovered.

"We'll camp here tonight," he told her, and began to start building a fire.

He caught fish from the sea and they ate and slept until the early morning light. A mist came in off the cold waters as they both woke, and they saw a man standing there. He was wearing a light brown cloak, with his long white hair combed neatly down the back of his neck, matching his thick white beard. This was Rosha.

Nicolea and Alexeena moved closer. "Welcome back, Nicolea Dan," Rosha said to him.

Nicolea nodded. "Hello Rosha." Then he climbed

onto the boat.

Alexeena hesitated, unsure of what was to come next.

Rosha smiled. "You are also expected, milady," he said to her. He gestured with his hand to guide her to the boat.

As the boat left the shores, the mist swallowed them up. Alexeena began to feel a slight tingling. Something was changing. Everything that had created the bio-tek part of her fell away into the deep sea below. She was now made to the image of what she was born with, the image of the Lord of Light. She looked up at Nicolea, and he just smiled at her. She smiled back.

A small, cold moon circled a large frozen planet. The star system's sun was small and dying. This small, cold moon was Mammon. No life existed on this moon. In fact, no life existed anywhere in the system, except for that which came in from outside. A large, black temple-like structure had been built on the moon, and it sat in contrast to the land and snow around it.

Coming into the thin atmosphere of this moon was the destroyer flagship Brimstone. It was Andrelus Pan's personal ship, and he stood on its bridge like the ruler he was. The Brimstone lowered slowly in the moon's sky, stopping to hover just over the temple. In the distance a winter lightning storm was moving in, and the snow was falling faster, becoming thick and heavy as the cold mist rolled in.

Once the destroyer completely stopped, a small shuttle, shaped much like a bat with small wings, left the docking port of the Brimstone and lowered itself down on one of the tall towers. A large hatchway opened from the top, and the shuttle entered straightway.

Deep within the temple was a large, darkened room lit only by ancient torches hanging on the walls around. Sitting in the middle of the room was a large bloodwood table built centuries in the past. Around the table sat five shadowed men, faces hidden in the darkness. A large stone staircase sat in one of the narrow ends of the room. It went up about fifteen steps, then split, continuing up on either side. Coming down one side was a cloaked Andrelus Pan. The sound of echoes rang around the room with each step he took.

He took his seat at the head. "The Black Star prison has been destroyed."

"It seems the Union of Light has suddenly found themselves a fleet of ships," said another voice from somewhere around the table.

"Have we found where they are holed up?" asked another voice.

"Their base has been found," replied Andrelus, "but now we have a fleet to find. I believe it is time to crack down on the citizens, make sure they are not aiding them. Some may have knowledge of the rebellious Union. This Union of Light is a threat."

"I say we start with the true believers of the Light." That was another voice. It was a deep voice, coming from the other end of the table. It caused Andrelus to look up and give a single nod.

Another voice piped in. "We need to increase funds and expand the Molokan Way to more cultures and cities in the empire."

"It's being expanded as we speak," said the deep voice in the dark.

"First we need to extinguish the Lord of Light and His influence across the galaxy," Andrelus replied after a moment of silence. "That should be our only goal, and all these other things just aide in that goal. Whatever you need to do to achieve this goal, do it."

There were mumbles and nods among the members of the table, who were in total agreement. Then the deep voice from the other end of the table spoke back up. It was obvious from everyone else's demeanor that this shadowed man was feared.

When he spoke, everyone listened. "What I want to know is, did any information leak out about this place, our ancient home, during the Black Star attack?"

"We don't think so," said one of the figures.

"But we need to know for sure," Andrelus piped in. "We have infiltrated the Union, which is how we found their base on Dust. We need to put in our own spies there, not sleepers."

"Then we can destroy them from the inside out," the deep-voiced man replied.

Everyone readily agreed. Then Andrelus said, "In the meantime, we need to continue to divide the people with racism and hatred. Make sure to use the universal propaganda through all sources of media. We don't want the people to hear what is really happening with the Union. If we can stop their support, we will be that much closer to their defeat."

"Everyone leave," spoke the deep voice. "I need to speak to Andrelus alone."

All the members of the shadow council stood up and left the room, heading back to their respective areas.

They knew the meeting was over, and they knew what they had to do.

Once alone, the dark-voiced man said, "With Thermonte dead, the Imperium needs a new face to blame when things go wrong."

"I will find us one."

"There is a man on one of the inner worlds who has the name of Corlesh," the hidden shadow replied. "He makes a living doing odd jobs so to speak."

Andrelus grinned. He remembered his own past. "Much like I used to do before I joined into the shadow."

"Urmm, yes," was the reply. "And this Corlesh does pretty much the same as you? Perhaps you could bring him into our way of thinking." This man sounded like the perfect candidate.

"That can be arranged." With that the deep-voiced man stood, slowly and feebly. Then Andrelus asked, standing himself, "Would you like any assistance?"

"I will be fine. This body is just a temporary possession, so I need to find a new one fast." Then he said, "Can we use Electrik's flesh for anything you think? Is it still in good condition?"

"I can have it brought to you also, if you like. I'm

sure you can rehydrate it somehow."

"Perhaps," replied the ancient figure. "Yes, bring it here. I may yet find some use for it."

"Well, at least you killed that Prophet Warrior," Andrelus replied, "so he will not be a threat to us anymore."

The old shadow huffed. "Be aware Andrelus Pan," he said. "Already another moves to take his place. Now go and find us a new leader and tighten the Imperium's hand."

Andrelus nodded, knowing there was nothing else to say. He made his way up to the landing platform and into his waiting shuttle. It lifted up and soared high, into the mouth of the Brimstone.

The Union had designated the Spearhead battleship Liberty their flagship, where the high command of the Union would gather. Grand Admiral Boone and General Brande sat in a room on the Liberty, waiting. Most of the Spearhead ships at the Utopian shipyards had been utilized but had been scattered across the known galaxy. The Union base on Dust had been pounded back to dust by the Pagonic destroyers. Luckily, most had survived the attack.

They were worried about the attack. Just how had the Imperium found their base? The person they were waiting on walked in. Jon Vega stood before them a different man. A man so different, he was probably the only man they could trust about this current situation. Jon had gotten clearance and had become an agent in the intelligence world for the Union and was given the rank of commander. And as soon as he had walked in, he knew something was up, and it wasn't good.

"We have some information we need you to find out for us, Jon," Brande began. He and Jon had always had worked well together in the past and seemed to have a good rapport with one another.

"Yes, sir," Jon answered, getting back in the routine of things.

"We need to find out if we have a traitor in our ranks, or anywhere in the Union."

Jon was taken aback. "A traitor?"

Admiral Boone nodded. "That's right. Somehow, the enemy found out about our base on Dust. If you find no traitor, then we'll have to assume that they had been looking and had gotten lucky."

Jon thought about this for a while. Surely no one would betray the Union, no one he had met. There was one other possibility, but he hated to think about it. "Perhaps there is another reason, a more simple one, if I may put it on the table?"

"By all means, Commander," Boone told him.

"Perhaps something had a tracking device, or someone, without knowing it was there."

The General and the Admiral looked at one another, then back at Jon. They motioned for him to continue.

"Since the Chimera was actually Thermonte's ship, perhaps it had one placed before we set out."

"Not likely, since we performed a thorough scan on it when you returned."

"Then maybe it was Soshiana. She was a bio-tek, after all. She may not have known it was there. She was put together by the enemy, according to her and her memories."

"Jon, we just found out that Thermonte Electrik was found dead just one day before the Imperial Tribute," Boone told him. "Cause of death was a blade embedded deep into his stomach. The last person to see him was a girl that fit Soshiana's description."

"She killed her former boss?"

Brande nodded. "Looks that way. So now we need you to find out if we have a traitor here in our service, that could have given the information to the empire."

Jon mentally gathered himself together. "I'll find out one way or another."

As Jon walked out of the room, Brande turned toward his counterpart and said, "I hope we're wrong about this."

"Me too."

CHAPTER THIRTEEN

Mission to Synoa

Saffron Baye woke in her cabin on board the New Haven Spearhead ship, now attached to the Ephesus. She was a grand admiral now, and her entire fleet was attached to the Ephesus for protection on the long journey. She knew this would be a long journey, one that she would not probably finish. She also knew it was her calling.

She sat up and rolled her feet onto the floor, standing up and stretching. She looked over at her holo-chronometer, which told her it was the morning according to Ephesus time. All of the ships were on the same time, keeping it all simple. Those that had once been fighting with the Union, and were now heading out with the Ephesus, had to adjust. It wasn't that hard, and nearly all the Union men there had gotten used to it within a week.

While the Ghel were appreciative of their escort, they were civilians, not soldiers. They preferred to not focus on the military presence in their daily lives. It was agreed that when one of the Union members was to come and visit within any one of the Ephesus' biospheres, no military uniform would be worn.

The Ghel people had settled into their living conditions. The first biosphere was named Imaelan, the middle was called Kamaelan, and the third biosphere was called Jamaelan. The names from their promised land on Bel Terra of course held great historical significance, but it was also prophesied that they would one day regain those lands.

It had been only a month since their departure, and there were many more hurdles to come, but Saffron was willing to see things through and to help get things set up.

After taking her shower, putting on her grand admiral uniform, and putting her hair up, she walked out of her cabin and headed toward the flight bridge of the New Haven. "Report," she said, as she walked onto the bridge.

"Nothing to report," said a night captain, in charge when most of the crew were sleeping. His name was

Kade Poe, once an Agent of the Republic from Del Argo. Kade had decided to travel with the escort fleet. She also had Charlie Dole from Jasper, now second in command of the armada.

"Quiet as always, eh?" was Saffron's response.

"I have a feeling we're in for a lot of those."

Saffron worked her shift, which was nothing to talk about. All was quiet and silent. She looked over the standard object reports, which were all about the surrounding space dust outside the ship, all of which was easily deflected by the light shields. She placed Captain Dole in charge, and left the bridge early. She was having dinner with a friend she had met on Dust. He and his family lived in the biosphere land of Jamaelan.

He was Jesse Boone, Solomon's brother.

Once back in her own cabin, she removed her uniform and took yet another shower. Then she dressed in a casual dress, such as the Ghel women would, and headed out into the portal lift, entering the Ephesus close to the front. She made her way out from the industrial area behind the walls and entered the land of Imalaen, then made her way to Imalaen Station One. The train came in and she stepped on the train just as it took off. Five minutes later, she was in the space tube heading into the middle biosphere. The space tube only took about two and a half minutes, but the view was incredible. She had always loved the beauty of being in space.

Five more minutes, and she reached Jamaelan Station One. Saffron left the station and headed down the road to the Boone household. She always tried to talk him into becoming a part of her team on the New Haven, but instead he had taken a job in the Jamaelan District as a Detective Local, which is what he had been on the world of Tiere. Of course, being one in the Jamaelan District would be much easier. Jesse would be able to spend more time with his family, which is what he wanted.

It was the reason he had moved to Dust, those many years ago.

There was one thing he would do for her. Jesse had a way to find out news about the war. At least, he would be able to for a couple of years. When she came over for dinner, they would contact Solomon Boone and get the official war news, so to speak. Saffron would give Solomon reports of the trip. Afterward, she would need to leave before the trains shut down for the night.

That night, Saffron came from her bathroom and

into her bedroom, thinking about her day. She sat down on her bed and thought about Jon, and wondered if she should send him a message through Solomon. She would decide later. She threw her feet under the bed coverings, the lights went out, and Saffron went to sleep.

The freighter Valcron came closer to Synoa Station, slowing down to wait their turn into the mining facility in the center of the field. The station pinged their identification and contacted them as they came in closer, slowing nearly to a stop. "Freighter Valcron, before gaining passage to the Synoa facility, please provide your purpose for entry."

"Synoa Station, we have a delivery for the central market from the planet Deveron. Twelve pallets of spices and meats. Mostly for the eateries there." That was the captain of the Valcron, a man named Sabat.

Standing behind him was Ben Gettel. He was on a secret mission to get some information from a sympathetic informant who worked in the mining facility. He stood with a bunch of the other crew members, listening to the communications between the captain and the station. Sabat and his crew were not only making a legal delivery, but were also picking up something illegal to take back to their main employer, a Mister Mal Corlesh. They were going to smuggle out a golden jewel found in one of the mines within the asteroid field.

"Valcron," replied the station, "sending you the coordinates to prepare for your entry into the tunnel. Once you are in position, send us confirmation and we will open the tunnel field."

"Confirmed," Sabat replied, and ordered his pilot to the coordinates.

The Valcron moved into position, the confirmation was sent, and the green light appeared from the facility, slowly maneuvering the rocks out of the way. When the tunnel had been opened, the Valcron began to slowly move into the green tunnel and down through it toward the facility. Twenty minutes later, they were out of the tunnel and in the safety zone surrounding the lithium facility. There they were instructed as to which bay they could enter, just above the loading bays.

"Alright," Sabat told his crew, "we have about twelve hours before we have to leave and the cargo is unloaded. They won't start unloading for another couple of hours, so Ben, I will need you back here by then. You are the new member, and you get that job."

Ben nodded. What he had to do would not take that long, he hoped. Once they were released, Ben made his way to the central market and found the restaurant called SHANTY'S PORT. He was to meet his informant there. He had never met the man before, but he had his orders so the informant would contact him.

He walked in and stood in the short line at the front to place his order. Once it was his turn, he ordered a tanglefish special, and went and sat down at one of the tables in the restaurant. Several minutes later, a man came out and handed him his food, then sat down across from him.

"You the Union man?" the man asked him. "I was told to see a Union man."

"Long live the Light," replied Ben, for that was the code that was agreed upon.

The man reached into a pocket from behind his apron, and handed Ben a small box. Ben took the box and opened it. It contained a small electronic chip about half the size of a fingernail. The man leaned in and spoke to him again.

"Connect it to your Nav-system, it will lead you where you need to go. It will unscramble the coordinates to Mammon." Then the man simply got up and made his way to the back.

Ben looked around and placed the box into his pocket. Then he sat and ate the food he ordered, which was surprisingly good. He hadn't actually known what a tanglefish was.

About thirty minutes later, he was up and heading back to the ship. Before he reached it, he noticed several Pagonic soldiers searching the ship, Sabat standing there letting them. Before anything could be done, Sabat looked over and saw Ben and pointed. The soldiers' eyes followed Sabat's arm and saw Ben, who backed away and then turned and ran back deeper into the facility. The soldiers chased him.

The captain of the soldiers stepped up to Sabat then and handed him a golden jewel for payment for his information. "The Imperium thanks you and Mister Corlesh for your cooperation." Sabat nodded and took the jewel, making his way back into the Valcron.

Ben knew there might be trouble, but he didn't expect to be sold out by the smugglers. Somehow he needed to get off the facility, but he wasn't sure how he was going to manage it. He had no plan and there was no backup. Somehow, he had been setup this whole time. Strangely enough, no alarms had sounded that he knew of, unless they were silent.

He circled down to another floor, leading down to the loading bay, where the tanker ships waited to be filled with lithium in solid form to be transported to the many different processing plants around the galaxy. The tanker ships themselves usually took at least three crew to run them. As he had made it down to the loading bay, local security had been notified that the Pagonic soldiers were looking for him.

He ran through a cluster of them, and they began to chase him and fire their weapons at him as he weaved in and out of the tankers. Ben had no weapon on him, as he was supposed to be undercover on his mission. But someone did, and seemed to be firing back at the security. Soon, he knew, soldiers would be joining them.

Ben made his way to the person firing back. "Need a little help, I see," she said, throwing him an x-20 rifle.

The woman who had thrown him the rifle climbed out of one of the tanker ships and stood next to him, leaning out from behind just enough to see what they were shooting at. She had straight, shoulder-length black hair. She was slender and wore an outfit you might find on a desert planet. She wore her blaster pistol on her hip and a Gravelgan-handled blade on her belt.

"Hi," was all that Ben could get out. Then he said, "I'm Ben."

"Ben Gettel," she said and smiled. "I know."

After a bit more fighting, Ben asked, "I don't think I know you?"

"I go by Alexeena," she replied.

Just then, the Pagonic soldiers stormed the loading bay. Alexeena told Ben, "I think its time we leave. This is my ship." She pointed to the tanker behind her. Come on, let's go."

Ben followed her onto her ship, and immediately she shouted orders to the other two of her crew. The tanker took off, but she was not attached to her lithium tank, and it was left behind.

"Are you hacked in?" she asked one of her crew.

"Ready to roll," replied the man, whose name was Simon.

Simon's wife, Nora, sat in the pilot's seat. She flew the tanker toward a cluster of smaller asteroids when Alexeena gave the order. The green tunnel activated and they entered.

"I don't know how long I can keep it opened, Nora, so you need to punch it," Simon shouted.

The tanker then made its jump while they were still in

the tunnel. It broke apart a bit of the green walls and the tunnel collapsed. Once they were safe, Alexeena turned toward her new passenger and asked, "You still don't recognize me, do you?"

"I'm sorry," he replied. "I don't."

She smiled again, and said, "It doesn't really matter. So, Ben, where do we need to take you?"

Ben just stared at her for a moment. He then recognized her from the base on Dust. He said, "Take me to the world of Korinth."

Author's Note

This is the second edition of the second book from the World of Strangers and Pilgrims. Not as much of this edition has changed, but there are changes. This book is mostly set twelve years after Conflict With Shadows. As the first book had many Christian elements in it, this one has many more stories from the Bible woven in. There are more installments of this series planned. I hope you have enjoyed reading these stories I as much as I have enjoyed writing them.

For those interested in history, you may find it fun to know that many of the names of ships and captains in the Union of Light fleet are inspired by real ships and their captains. These names were taken from steamboats that traveled the Missouri river in the past.

This is a Christian Science Fiction book, written primarily for teens and young adults, and you will find some Biblically-inspired stories within the larger tale. There will never be any foul language or inappropriate scenes that would compromise the Christian lifestyle. There is one character in these stories that does represent the world's newest take on self-representation as something other that she was born as. As some of our characters will find, there is always hope. No matter your walk in life, there is hope for you, too. I have included the Romans Road to salvation as a starting point. I would suggest you go to your local church and talk to someone there about this road.

The greatest road anyone will ever travel: The Romans Road of Salvation

Romans 3:23 KJV "For all have sinned, and come short of the glory of God;"

Romans 6:23 KJV "For the wages of sin *is* death; but the gift of God *is* eternal life through Jesus Christ our Lord."

Romans 5:8 KJV "But God commendeth his love toward us, in that, while we were yet sinners, Christ died for us."

Romans 10:9 KJV "That if thou shalt confess with thy mouth the Lord Jesus, and shalt believe in thine heart that God hath raised him from the dead, thou shalt be saved."

Romans 10:13 KJV "For whosoever shall call upon the name of the Lord shall be saved."

Romans 8:1 KJV "*There is* therefore now no condemnation to them which are in Christ Jesus, who walk not after the flesh, but after the Spirit."

Romans 8:38-39 KJV "For I am persuaded, that neither death, nor life, nor angels, nor principalities, nor powers, nor things present, nor things to come, nor height, nor depth, nor any other creature, shall be able to separate us from the love of God, which is in Christ Jesus our Lord."

ABOUT THE AUTHOR

Mark Castleberry has been a fan of science fiction and fantasy fan since childhood. He grew up on a lake in Alabama, wanting to write since high school. All the characters and stories have been lodged in his head for many years and writing them down for most of his life never having anything published, until the internet opened up and self-publishing began an option. He met his future wife at his job, and followed her to Missouri to marry her. Now he resides in Missouri with his wife and two cats. He now writes a very imaginatively, fast-paced series of books and stories with Christian influences that just may leave you breathless. His books contain Christian morals and values, and the tales weaved into it come from the Bible.

In addition to writing books and stories for the young adult audience, he runs the Stranger and Pilgrims Podcast, which host old time radio stories and audio dramas that can open up your imagination. You can follow the author on several social media sites as well as his website at www.strangerspilgrims.com

EDITORIAL REVIEW

Into Shadow's Fire is a work of fiction in the science fiction, action, and adventure subgenres and serves as the second installment in the World of Strangers and Pilgrims series. It is suitable for the general reading audience and was penned by author Mark Castleberry. The book continues the journey of Jon Vega and Nicolea Dan a decade after the events of the previous installment. Now a part of the Union of Light, they must help the people of Sulia who are being persecuted on religious grounds by the Pagonic Imperium. As they plan to flee to the stars, the Empire prepares to do everything it can to stop them.

Like a lot of great science fiction, this book is an allegory for the world around us and wastes no time in exploring the subjects of faith and religious persecution. Mark Castleberry's writing will quickly resonate with a great many readers, shining a light on the experience of having to flee for your life because your faith offends the regime in which you live. These themes are explored in the beautiful world that the author has created, a stunning and creative universe that serves as the perfect backdrop to this story. The tale of Thermonte was expertly woven into the wider narrative to help expand the world of the story and create a deeper and more nuanced understanding of the threat the people of Sulia faced, aided in no small part by Thermonte's excellent characterization. Overall, Into Shadow's Fire is a worthy entry into the series and continues pushing the saga toward its powerful message.

<u>Also By The Author:</u>

THE WAY OF CAIN AND JONAH'S RUN

<u>**THE WORLD OF STRANGERS AND PILGRIMS SERIES**</u>

1. CONFLICT WITH SHADOWS
2. INTO SHADOW'S FIRE
3. SHADOW'S WINTER

Published by Strangers and Pilgrims Publishing
www.strangerspilgrims.com